D0295620

Books should be returned or renewed by the
last date stamped above

_____

_____

_____

Awarded for excellence

C152454087

Trouble
in the
Amen Corner

Trouble in the Amen Corner

Amusing and heartwarming
tales of a small
Cornish town at War

Betty Kellar

ISIS
LARGE PRINT
Oxford

First published in Great Britain 2000
by
Peter Tuffs

Published in Large Print 2005 by ISIS Publishing Ltd,
7 Centremead, Osney Mead, Oxford OX2 0ES
by arrangement with the author

British Library Cataloguing in Publication Data
Kellar, Betty
   Trouble in the amen corner. – Large print ed.
   (Isis reminiscence series)
   1. World War, 1939–1945 – personal narratives,
   British
   2. World War, 1939–1945 – Social
   aspects – England – Cornwall
   3. Large type books
   I. Title
   940.5'3161'092

ISBN 0–7531–9994–7 (hb)
ISBN 0–7531–9995–5 (pb)

Printed and bound by Antony Rowe, Chippenham

Dedication

To Alan, my husband, who shares with me both the hard work and the pleasure.

Preface

Although these events happened well over fifty years ago, they are true as I remember them. Sometimes it was difficult to remember them in the right order, so whenever possible I checked contemporary newspapers now stored on microfilm in Plymouth Reference Library. I am grateful to the staff there who helped me and also to the war-time reporters of the *Western Morning News* and *Evening Herald*, whose work is preserved there. The characters in this book all existed but I have changed their names and jumbled them up to preserve their anonymity. Tales of my family are unaltered. My sisters are quite happy at this and I know my Mum would have been. But Gan . . . ? I expect she is as exasperated with me, from the Other Side, as she was on this one.

Trouble in the Amen Corner

"There'll be trouble in the Amen Corner!" was one of Gan's many sayings, but she had no idea of where the Amen Corner was.

A check in the *Oxford English Dictionary* showed that it was an American phrase which described a Corner in some Protestant churches, near the pulpit. The Corner was occupied by particularly devout believers and their fervent cries of "Amen" would support everything said by the preacher.

The connection between that and Gan's use of it seems rather obscure, but *she* knew what she meant.

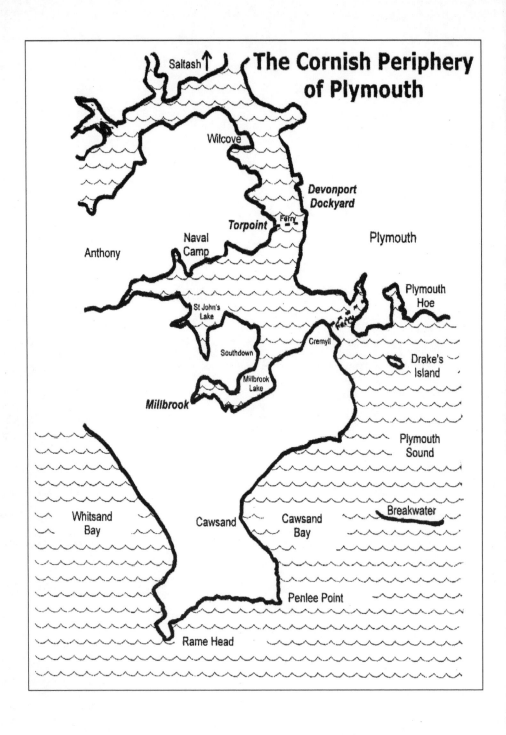

The Cornish Periphery of Plymouth

Saltash ↑

Wilcove

Devonport Dockyard

Torpoint

Ferry

Naval Camp

Anthony

Plymouth

St John's Lake

Plymouth Hoe

Southdown

Cremyll

Ferry

Millbrook Lake

Drake's Island

Millbrook

Plymouth Sound

Breakwater

Whitsand Bay

Cawsand

Cawsand Bay

Penlee Point

Rame Head

CHAPTER
ONE

"Be Patriotic! Use a big sponge and a little water!"
(From a women's wartime magazine)

In 1942, people were asked to use no more than five
inches of water in their baths, to save fuel.

By the time my family moved from the Cornish village
of Millbrook in 1942 to Torpoint, just across the Tamar
from Devonport, our social position had definitely improved.

The previous move from a dilapidated cottage in
Millbrook to one considerably less so, had been on the
back of Mr Dobson's rag-and-bone handcart. This
time, we travelled less conspicuously in the back of
Dicken's delivery van, to a bay-windowed flat in Torpoint.

My grandmother, whom we called Gan, had started
off in an ebullient mood.

"Thank Heaven to be away from all those
quarrelsome neighbours," she exclaimed, as we
bumped along the narrow, high-hedged lane out of
Millbrook. "Just because I had given one or two of
them a piece of my mind!"

Unfortunately, her distribution of pieces of her mind
had been overgenerous. The result was that our family
left Millbrook with an uncomfortable suspicion that
some people were glad to see the back of us.

1

At least, that was how Mum, my sister Diane and I felt, our skins always several layers thinner than Gan's. My youngest sister Jill, at five (Diane and I were aged ten and eleven), was too young to feel mortification. She clung tightly to Mum as the van tipped us round sharp bends and up steep hills, her mind entirely occupied with staying on the narrow bench-seat behind the driver.

I think Mr Dicken must have been in a hurry. We reached Torpoint in record time, but Jill had banged her head on the van-side and was crying, I was feeling sick, and Gan had lost her good humour.

"Don't give him a tip, Ida," she hissed at Mum while Mr Dicken was unloading our possessions in Clarence Road. She then took exception to the length of time Mum spent behind the van with him, before Mr Dicken drove away, wreathed in smiles.

The van was hardly out of sight, before recriminations began to flash between Mum and Gan. For some reason Gan didn't believe Mum's indignant denials that she had given Mr Dicken anything more than his stipulated fee.

"Then why did he look so pleased with himself, tell me that?" Gan demanded, then stopped abruptly when she saw us children anxiously watching her.

"Here, carry this in between you," she snapped, thrusting the suitcase at Diane and me. "And you can shut up," she turned on a still whimpering Jill. "It didn't kill you."

She didn't say another word to Mum but she didn't need to. Her stiffened figure and Mum's high colour told us all too plainly that they were still at loggerheads. The atmosphere lightened as we inspected our new home. Mum liked the size of the rooms, after our tiny cottage ones, while Gan's chief approval was for the back garden. There was nothing in it but a long paved path to the back gate, with a fence along the side dividing it from the house next door, and an Anderson shelter with rough grass growing on top of it.

"That's to camouflage it from German planes," she told us. "Thank the Lord no-one will expect us to grow potatoes in that."

My sisters and I were exhilarated at our first experience of electric lights, after the oil-lamp-lit cottage in Millbrook. We kept switching them on and off until Gan caught us at it.

"You little blighters," she shouted at us. "What are you playing at? Who do you think's going to pay for that?" It hadn't occurred to us that anyone would have to pay for it. "We have to put shillings in a meter, and if we run out of money it'll be back to the oil-lamp."

The relief of leaving behind in Millbrook all the people Gan had quarrelled with was a bonus. Our main reason for moving to Torpoint was its proximity to Devonport Dockyard, where Mum worked.

She had faced a long, often uncomfortable journey each day between Millbrook and Devonport. Millbrook lay at the head of a tidal creek. At low tide the small ferry could not reach the village and at those times Mum had to be up at five in the morning to catch it lower down the creek. In the winter months she crossed the estuary in the dark, often in wild, wet weather.

3

Old Mr Brown, one of the few neighbours in Millbrook Gan had not fallen out with (he was deaf), had warned Mum of the risks of moving nearer the Dockyard.

"You'll be taking your little family into danger," he had told her. "Them Germans are always aiming at Plymouth and Devonport." But Mum and Gan were convinced that the worst of the bombing was over.

We had been in our new home for an hour or so, when our upstairs neighbour came to the door with a tray of tea. Mrs Shipley was a pretty, fair-haired woman, with a friendly London accent.

"Thought you'd be gasping," she said cheerfully. "There's nothing like a cuppa to buck you up." She had a shy little boy hanging behind her. "Come and say hullo, Peter," she coaxed and Peter did, though without letting go of his mother's skirt.

Mrs Shipley politely declined an invitation to come in and immediately gained Gan's approval.

"It's better not to be too friendly with neighbours," she stated, after she had closed the door behind Mrs Shipley and Peter. "That's when trouble starts." In fact, trouble started in less than a week, though it was a little longer before Mrs Shipley realised it.

After the tiny cottage windows in Millbrook, the large ones in the flat caused us real blackout problems. The question of the bedroom windows was solved by Gan removing the single, overhead light bulb. We crept in and out of our beds in the dark. And since "front room" meant "best room", we never used it. Gan's kitchen blackout solution was a blanket, removed from the double bed she and Mum shared and replaced when they retired each night.

Mrs Shipley came to the back door one day, at the early winter blackout time, just as Gan had climbed onto a chair with the blanket.

"Pringle's have got some safety pins in," she had come to tell us. "One packet per customer until stocks run out. And they probably will have by the morning." She became aware of Gan, struggling to hook the heavy blanket over the curtain rail.

"You could do with some curtain tape to sew on that, Mrs Cooper. I've got a couple of yards you can have, if you don't mind unpicking it off an old curtain. Then you could cut the blanket down the middle and that would make it easier to draw."

Too proud to admit to the blanket's dual purpose, Gan resorted to disdain. "Thank you, Mrs Shipley, but it wouldn't be worth wasting tape and thread on this old blanket." She gave it a careless flick of her fingers, before stepping off the chair with straight-backed dignity. "It'll do as it is until we get something more suitable. And I'm alright for pins, thank you. I can let you have some if you're still short."

So Mrs Shipley left, slightly deflated, with two large safety pins and three small ones from Gan's dwindling stock, a suitably grateful recipient when she had come as a giver.

She had scarcely closed the door behind her when Gan said irritably, "She needn't think she's coming down here to brag about her spare curtains." Diane and

Mrs Shipley came to the back door, just as Gan had climbed onto a chair with the blanket.

I exchanged uneasy glances. We recognised the early signs of a fall-out even if Mrs Shipley hadn't.

There were more ominous signs of trouble to come, when Mrs Shipley generously offered us the use of her bath once a week. On her way out shopping, dressed in a smart new coat, she knocked on our kitchen door and caught Gan in the middle of washing, her sleeves rolled up to her elbows, and a damp apron tied round her middle.

Mrs Shipley explained her mission. "So if you'd like to come up every Thursday after tea, Mrs Cooper, you're welcome . . . as long as you bring your own soap. Did you hear, there's a rumour it's going to be rationed? And don't forget . . . only five inches of water!" As the pungent smell of wet clothes mixed with bubble-and-squeak reached her nose, she said brightly, "Something smells nice, Mrs Cooper. It makes me feel quite hungry."

"Yes, I'm giving the girls their dinner before they go back to school," Gan said, pointedly.

"Oh, I won't keep you then. So is that all right? Thursday evenings? It's difficult enough keeping kids clean. Peter gets so grubby, I don't know what I'd do without a bath to pop him in."

Seated round the kitchen table, waiting for our bubble-and-squeak we could see Gan's back stiffen. Her politeness, what we called her posh voice, though not in her hearing, intensified.

"Thanks all the same, but we wouldn't dream of troubling you, Mrs Shipley," she said graciously. "Boys are different to girls. You can't keep them out of the dirt. Our girls don't get dirty. They wouldn't dare! And yes, I did hear that soap will go on ration soon. Luckily I've got a good stock of it, so if you're short, I can help you out. And now, you'll have to excuse me, or the girls will be late for school."

So once again Gan, unable to accept a kindness with grace, countered it with an offer of her own. Our years of poverty had enlarged the chip on her shoulder to such an extent that she was always on the defensive.

I heard Gan telling Mum the tale when she came home from the Dockyard that evening.

She fumed, "Fancy having the nerve to suggest our girls weren't clean! Just let her come down again with any of her aspersions."

Mum had flopped wearily into a chair at the table. "I'm sure she was only trying to be helpful," she said, but with little conviction because she knew Gan would not believe it.

Gan snorted. "Helpful, my eye! She just wanted to swank because they've got a bathroom and we haven't." Preoccupied though she was with her righteous indignation, Gan could not miss Mum's tired face. She poured her a cup of tea. "Here, get this down you," she said gruffly. "What sort of a day have you had?"

All Mum's working days were hard. She stood, hour after hour, at a huge machine in Devonport Dockyard, drilling holes in ships' side plates. Although she had got over the early days, when worry over her job became nightmares to rack her sleep, she still came home physically exhausted.

8

Mum gratefully gulped down the hot, strong tea. "As a matter of fact, I had half-an-hour's lie down this afternoon," she told us. "We had a practice invasion and I had to be one of the dead bodies."

"Well that sounds pessimistic," Gan retorted. "Did you have dead Germans too?"

"I don't know," Mum admitted. "But Debbie was put out because she had to be a 'walking-wounded' and stagger round with her leg in a splint, while I just had to lie in the road and wait to be carried off on a stretcher. Debbie said she wouldn't have minded but she had to wait forty minutes before she could go to the lav."

Debbie was on the drilling machine next to Mum's. She was a robust young Plymouth woman, who had taken over her husband's job in the Dockyard when he was called up into the Navy. She and Mum became unlikely friends, her outgoing character attracted to Mum's gentle diffidence. Debbie had a vulgar sense of humour. She told Mum all sorts of ribald tales which Mum repeated to Gan with a kind of shocked enjoyment.

The telling of these tales meant Mum and Gan, if we children were within earshot, resorting to their secret language. What they did not realise was that I had cracked their code some months earlier, so that Diane and I now knew that they were simply taking the initial sounds off key words and tagging them onto the end.

So when Mum went on, "Debbie was telling me a funny story about her hubby, when he was home on leave last week," she looked at my interested face,

She stood, hour after hour, at a huge drilling machine in
Devonport Dockyard.

before continuing. "They'd had a row one morning about . . . you know . . . and he asked her if she anted-w it on a ate-pl."

"Anted-w it on a ate-pl?" Gan repeated slowly, while I thought, "Wanted it on a plate . . . what's funny about that?"

Mum said, "It . . . you know . . ."

"It . . . you don't mean his . . . ?"

"Yes," chuckled Mum. "So Debbie said yes, that's what she did want, just for a joke. And that's what she got. He ave-g it to her on a ate-pl, with her toast."

Gan said, incredulous, "Surely not on the same plate?" "Good Lord, no." Mum sounded quite shocked before she added slowly, "Surely not." I gave Diane a surreptitious glance. She was as puzzled as I was. Despite having broken Mum and Gan's code, we were often none the wiser. But Gan obviously saw the point because she broke into cackles of laughter, quite forgetting her irritation with the lady upstairs.

But only for a while. Things came to a head between the two women when they had a fall-out over the air-raid shelter.

There was a late evening air attack on Devonport and we went to the shelter in the garden. It was cold and miserable inside, with a damp, musty smell, and the only light we had was from Mum's camouflaged torch.

As we sat in the gloom, listening to gunfire taking over from the last wail of the siren, Gan said, "I wonder why the Shipleys' haven't come down?"

11

Mum was hesitant. "Perhaps they don't feel they'd be welcome."

"Nonsense," Gan answered her sharply. "They've as much right in this shelter as we have."

We all sat for a while without a word. We could hear a solitary plane droning above us, but for once Gan did not tell us whether it was one of ours or one of theirs. Instead, she sprang to her feet.

"I'm going to fetch them," she suddenly announced, and was gone before Mum had managed more than a gasp of remonstration.

She was gone for ages. Mum became restless, torn between going to look for her and leaving us. She breathed an audible sigh of relief when Gan returned as abruptly as she had left.

She peered over Gan's shoulder. "They haven't come down then?"

Gan flung herself down onto the bunk bed on which Diane and I sat. Even in the dark, and despite the distractions outside, we knew instantly that she was annoyed.

She hissed, "I'll swing for that woman. Do you know what she had the nerve to tell me? She said they never bothered to come down to the shelter; that raids here were nothing compared to the London Blitz! I told her, she should have been here last Spring, when poor old Plymouth and Devonport were flattened. And then when I started telling her about the plane that machine-gunned us in Millbrook, she came out with some long tale about when an incendiary bomb came through their roof. I said, we know all about being bombed, we were bombed out by a Zeppelin in the First World War!"

Her fierce competitiveness began to infect me. I said eagerly, "I bet they never had any German prisoners in their police station."

"Don't you believe it," Gan snorted. "She wouldn't even let me finish that one before she was spinning some yarn about someone she knew finding a German airman in her garden and bringing him in for a cup of tea! I tell you, she wouldn't let me get a word in edgeways."

Mum said weakly, "She might have just been glad to have someone to talk to, Mum. It must be lonely for her at night, alone with Peter, while her husband's away." She was squashed, as she so often was, by Gan's inexorable belief that she was always in the right.

"Nonsense! She's just one of those women who always have to go one better than everyone else." If Mum saw the irony of Gan's words, she would never have dared to say so. "Well, I told her we knew a man who rowed out to sea in a boat with a hole in it, to rescue a German airman, and even she couldn't beat that!"

The gunfire had gradually died down, after the last sporadic bursts hastening the enemy bombers back across the Channel. As the All Clear sounded we thankfully crept out of the shelter, to see a solitary searchlight still combing the sky. The raid had been nothing compared to others we had known. Of far greater significance was the apprehension that had hit each of us, except Jill, who was too young to recognise a familiar theme. Gan was once again at odds with a neighbour.

CHAPTER
TWO

Eyes in the Blackout — thanks to
Dr Carrot (Ministry of Food.)

That was the end of Gan's initial approval of Mrs Shipley. For a fair while, the two women kept out of each other's way and when they did meet, it was with an icy politeness on Gan's part and a wary reserve on Mrs Shipley's. We were not allowed to play with Peter. "We've got more than our fair share of kids," was Gan's firm opinion, for which, not unnaturally, we had no answer.

The next door neighbours were a middle-aged couple. Gan met them long before we did, and our first impressions of them were somewhat dubiously gained through her.

"They're very nice," she told us. "Mrs Crisp especially, is a much better-class person." She did not say who Mrs Crisp was better-class than, but we guessed she meant Mrs Shipley when she recounted with some satisfaction, "Mrs Crisp thinks Mrs Shipley comes from a very poor area of London, and we should make allowances."

The Crisps had two children. Their daughter was in the A.T.S. and when Gan found out that their son was a prisoner-of-war, sympathy was added to her general approval. They also had a little dog called Pip.

Mrs Crisp and Gan shared another interest. They both followed the Ministry of Food's continual advice on how to make do on the Kitchen Front, with equal zeal.

Apart from patriotism, which they shared, the two women were differently motivated. Mrs Crisp was deeply influenced by thoughts of her son.

"He was in a convoy, coming across the Atlantic," she said simply. "Bringing us food. And with his ship sunk under him and so many other boys lost — how could I ever condone waste, Mrs Cooper?"

While Gan wholeheartedly agreed with Mrs Crisp's sentiments, her own motivation included a more practical element. We were still hard up, despite Mum's job, for the bleak poverty in which we had existed for so long could not be instantly eradicated. Money went on higher rent and fuel costs . . . there was not the opportunity to collect and burn wood as there had been in Millbrook. It had to purchase a few extra pieces of second-hand furniture and weekly instalments in a clothing club had to be paid. The next priority was entertainment. It was such joy to be able to afford a new battery for the radio when we needed it, and to escape more frequently into the exciting world of the cinema.

Entertainment came before food, as Gan continued to provide the same scratch meals as she had in Millbrook, and we continued to ravenously eat everything she put in front of us. So when Lord

16

Woolton urged housewives to base all their meals on potatoes, which, he assured them, provided more energy than meat, and to use carrots, which helped people to see in the blackout, Gan was one of his most faithful followers. She grumbled at his presumption. "What does he know about cooking?" she demanded, scornfully. "I bet his wife doesn't let him anywhere near her kitchen." But when the Ministry of Food published recipes for meatless pies made with potato pastry, and orangeless marmalade made out of carrots, Gan set to in the kitchen, perhaps not with enthusiasm but certainly with a glow of satisfaction. She was not only helping to win the war, she was being economical at the same time.

She went further, often "improving" on Lord Woolton's recipes. After studying a recipe for Carrot Cookies one day, she announced, "I'm not going to waste my time spooning out all those fiddling little dollops. I'll double it and make it in a slab cake."

She got out a large baking tin and began to collect her ingredients.

"Carrots, eight tablespoons, grated. Betty, go and look in the drawer for the grater. Two ounces of marge. Four tablespoons of sugar . . . hmm. Pass me those saccharins, Diane, it'll have to be half-and-half. Twelve ounces of flour . . . I'll put in a bit less flour and a few more carrots. Have you found that grater yet?"

"It's not there," I said. Gan greeted this with an exasperated snort. "Why is it always me who has to find

17

things in this house?" She hurried over to the knife drawer, looking where I had looked and did not find it.

"That settles it! Grating's a waste of time, anyway. It'll taste better in slices."

We watched as Gan hacked the carrots into little lumps, then mixed everything up with a wooden spoon. I looked at the recipe. "It says a few drops of vanilla or orange flavouring," I said and immediately nettled her.

"A good cake doesn't need extra flavours added," she sharply told me. "It has enough of its own."

When she gave us each a piece of the cooked cake for tea, we thought it was marvellous. Thick and solid, with the carrots tasting just like apricots . . . that was what Gan said and since we had never tasted apricots we took her word for it . . . it was immediately satisfying. Even I could not manage a second slice.

The following morning, which was a Saturday, Gan wrapped up a piece of her cake in a brown paper bag and sent me round to Mrs Crisp with it. "Tell her, it's a variation on Lord Woolton's Carrot Cookies," she said rather grandly.

Mrs Crisp greeted me kindly, as she always did. On receiving the cake and Gan's message she exclaimed, "Well, fancy that! I made some myself yesterday. Wait a minute, Betty."

She bustled inside, to emerge with a bag of her own, which she gave to me. "You give this to your Gran and tell her . . . exchange is no robbery."

18

Gan did not seem too pleased to receive the little bag of cakes. She gave each of us children one and watched us closely as we ate them. We did not make the mistake of praising them but poor Mum, through a misunderstanding, was not so lucky.

We had arranged to meet Mum in Devonport, outside the Forum, at the end of her shift at the Dockyard. In the long queue noisily waiting to see Arthur Askey, Mum said, "I'm starving! They were short of supplies in the canteen today. What have you brought to eat, Mum?"

Gan had brought two bags of generously thick sandwiches, one lot filled with blackberry jam, the other with reconstituted dried egg. She had slices of her carrot cake and a bag of Mrs Crisp's cookies.

She took a cookie out of the bag and gave it to Mum. "Tell me what you think of these," she said. There was a defensive tone in her voice. Unfortunately, Mum took the wrong cue.

She bit into the little cake and exclaimed, "They're lovely, Mum."

At eleven years old I had become something of an ingratiate where Gan was concerned, born out of the intimidation she instilled in us. I stammered, "They're the s-s-same recipe as the s-s-slab cake, aren't they Gan? But the slab cake's better because you can taste all the little . . . little . . . l-l-lumps of carrot in it."

Mum firmly put her foot in it. "Well I think these are even better than the slab cake. Can I have another one, Mum?"

Turning an outraged back to us, Gan began a dignified shuffle forward with the queue, as the cinema doors opened.

With an angry snort, Gan thrust the bag at her. "Here, take the lot," she snapped, then turning an outraged back to us, she began a dignified shuffle forward with the queue, as the cinema doors opened. Mum cast me a helpless, interrogative look but there was no way I could answer it.

Mum and Gan did not have many rows, at least, not in front of us. But without anything being said, we knew that Mum was as afraid of Gan as we children were. Gan always got her own way until, one weekend that winter, Mum suddenly produced a most bizarre way of winning arguments.

Gan had a strong belief in Spiritualism, the occult, reading tea-leaves and a crystal ball. Strangest of all was her conviction, which we all took quite seriously, that

Baroness Orczy's fictional character, Sir Percy Blakeney, alias The Scarlet Pimpernel, had really existed, and was now in the spiritual world recruiting more followers to his League.

She had a list of this League in a little red book and kept adding names to it. Shot-down air aces joined it, soldiers who had shown conspicuous bravery and men who had gone down with their ships. And added to the list as honorary member was each of our names, so we too had to be brave.

Whether it was singing through air raids or gritting our teeth through her rough and ready ministrations to festering knees and septic fingers, facing a flock of belligerent geese or the real possibility of being invaded by the Germans, it was all the same to Gan. She refused to accept cowardice from us. "Don't let Sir Percy hear you cry," she would sternly order us, and we did not dare. Even poor little Jill, having a milk tooth pulled out by Gan with a piece of string, let the tears roll silently down her cheeks. Somehow or other, Sir Percy's influence was all the more potent for us not knowing exactly where he was. We only knew he was always watching us.

One Sunday morning, Gan burnt a pan of porridge . . . really burnt it, so that even she was hard put to it to retrieve anything edible from the mass of thick brown lumps in the saucepan. She dropped a dollop of it into each of our bowls, and covered it with a liberal amount of milk. "Get that down you," she ordered. "A few burnt bits won't do you any harm." She poured a cup of tea for Mum and herself.

Jill and I ate ours. She and I really did eat anything, we must have had stomachs of cast-iron. But Diane could not face hers. "I'm not hungry," she said, and pushed it away.

We all cast nervous glances at Gan, expecting an explosion, and we got one. She banged her hand on the table so that the pots shook.

"I am not throwing away good food, not in wartime. You'll eat it now or have it later for your dinner."

Diane burst into tears and Jill began to join her while I took the coward's way out and kept my head down. Mum suddenly jumped up from her chair and went to the sideboard. She came back with a note-pad and pencil.

Her expression was so serious, we all stared at her. Gan asked in a hushed tone, "Is it . . .?" and Mum gravely nodded her head.

As we watched her she began to write in a quick agitated script. From left to right her pencil scribbled furiously. She never lifted it from the page but swept it back in a continuous, heavy stroke, to begin each line of scribble. In the hushed atmosphere around the kitchen table, Mum stopped writing, lifted her head to look at Gan and said gently, "Sir Percy says, 'Let be, m'dear. Forget the porridge, pack up a picnic and go out. It's what you all need.'"

To our utter amazement, Gan's anger had evaporated like a pricked bubble. She got up from the table, with a gruff but subdued, "I'll make the sandwiches while you clear up, Ida. You kids, go and find your thick things, there's a cold wind blowing in from the sea."

We walked out of Torpoint to Wilcove, where the oil tanks had been set on fire the previous year, lighting up the Dockyard across the river for night after night of enemy bombing. Gan was right about the wind. Hidden in the cove were warships at anchor, pitching and rolling in the heavy swell.

As in all our winter picnics, we ate as we walked, dried-egg sandwiches, jam and some of Diane's favourites, cream-cracker sandwiches. On the way back we found some dried twigs and leaves in the hedges and collected them to burn on the fire, always a satisfaction. But over all, I could not get over this latest intervention of Sir Percy in our lives. For the first time ever, it had seemed he was on our side and not Gan's.

It was wash-night on Sundays, after tea, a proper wash-down at the sink in the scullery instead of what Gan called the cat's licks which sufficed every other night. We did not use the tin bath any more, which was a relief to me since the water in it had always been third-hand by the time it was my turn.

But it was cold in the scullery and we often rushed it. Gan would sometimes come and check we were not missing bits. She always seemed more concerned with our necks than anything else. To go to school with a dirty neck was a social stigma almost as bad as having nits in your hair.

There was a shortage of soap that winter and people swapped all sorts of ideas for making what they had go further. We were never sure whether Gan had got her ideas from someone else or had made them up herself, but it was all the same to us. If Gan said we had to wash in salt and vinegar, that is what we did . . . a sprinkling of one and a spoonful of the other and she said we did not need soap.

Tea was another soap substitute. In fact, tea seemed to serve numerous purposes, besides providing the cup that cheered. Not that we ever had much tea left in the pot, and when Mrs Crisp told Gan that cold tea was excellent for washing paintwork, she gave a snort of derision . . . after Mrs Crisp had gone.

"Fancy wasting good tea like that," she exclaimed. "All paintwork needs is a damp cloth and a bit of elbow grease."

A soapless week in 1942 was a different matter. At the end of the day she watered the pot and gave us a

She watered the pot and gave us a bowlful
of warm tea to wash in.

warm bowlful to wash our faces in. "It's an old custom," she said firmly, when Diane and I looked at one another askance. "It's better for your skin than soap. And what was good enough for your great-grandma is good enough for you." She then mixed the wet tea-leaves with coal dust and some sticky earth out of the garden, and formed the resulting horrible looking dough into brickettes for the fire.

A much nicer soap substitute was oatmeal, sprinkled into the washing water, making it milky. But there was nothing as coveted as the real thing.

Mrs Shipley came back from a visit to her London relatives and knocked on our door with an olive branch.

"Could you do with a tablet of Lifebuoy, Mrs Cooper?" she smiled. "The chemist was bombed at the end of my Auntie Flo's street and people were digging packets of it out of the rubble."

Gan was delighted. "I'd just about give my eye-teeth for one," she said feelingly. "We've been washing in tea all week. Thank you, Mrs Shipley, and it's nice to see you back."

Without apparently noticing Mrs Shipley's startled expression, she said quickly, "Can you spare a minute?" and hurrying to the cake tin on the sideboard, she got a knife and sawed vigorously into the cake, hacking off a generous slice. She put it onto a plate and gave it to Mrs Shipley. "Here, take this for your tea," she smiled. "It's some of my extra-special carrot cake. The kids can't tell it from apricot."

CHAPTER
THREE

"There was Bread, Bread,
just like lumps of Lead."

(From the wartime song, "Quartermaster's Store")

Diane and I started at our new school as soon as we arrived in Torpoint. Jill would not be old enough until the Autumn term. Unlike our Millbrook school, the classes were of mixed boys and girls, and the excitement must have gone to our heads. Within our first week there, we had joined Slogger Sloane's gang, and were joining in their mad rampage around the school yard every playtime. In that same week the

We had to stand in front of the class with outstretched hands,
while Miss Samson moved along the line with her cane.

whole gang, including two normally shy and now horror-stricken new girls, had to stand in front of the class with outstretched hands while Miss Samson, the headmistress, moved along the line with her cane.

Our faces must have roused her pity. When it was my turn she said severely, "I'm going to let you two off this time, since you are new, but make sure I don't find you here again," and missed out me and Diane to land a stinging whack on the hand of the boy next to us.

Not surprisingly, Slogger and his gang turned against us and our brief, reflected glory as friends of the top-dogs, turned into the torment of the hunted. Slogger and his friends waited for us after school and chased us up the back street to our flat.

Gan was out in the backyard collecting the washing one day, as Diane and I burst in, red-faced and gasping for breath. We got no sympathy from her.

She peered out of the back gate, in time to see Slogger and two of his cronies skulking round the corner, and came back in disbelief. "Why, they're only half your size," she castigated me. I was several inches taller than Diane. "Stand up to them, for Heaven's sake! They're only trying to put the wind up you."

After that, Slogger and his gang's persecution of us fizzled out. Either they found a more satisfying occupation, or the sight of Gan standing at the gate, arms akimbo, had frightened them off. Diane and I had learned a lesson. We realised that we were not cut out for gangs and canings and being chased home each afternoon. Thankfully, we slunk out of the limelight, back into a dull but safe obscurity.

Air-raids at our new school were very different affairs to the Millbrook ones. There, we had been expected to sit quietly in the cellars beneath the school, and carry on with our work. At Torpoint, the teachers were more indulgent. As soon as the siren started they hurried us to the shelters at the far side of the playground, and for the whole of the raid we sang noisy, cheerful songs, like "One man went to mow" and "Underneath the Spreading Chestnut Tree", or clapped our way through "Deep in the Heart of Texas".

These were special shelter songs, not to be confused with the songs we sang in the classroom. There was a strong music ethic in the school, cultivated by Miss McKenzie, who was Diane's teacher but who taught the whole school her wide repertoire of Scottish songs and English ballads. We sang sweet, plaintive tunes like the "Eriskay Love Lilt" or "Who is Sylvia?", or the stirring march of the "Hundred Pipers".

Miss McKenzie had a fiancé who was an Army officer and whenever he was on leave he came to her classroom. We thought it was wonderfully romantic. He always asked for "Ho Ro, My Nut-Brown Maiden", and sat gazing at Miss McKenzie at the piano, we were sure with his heart in his eyes, as we sang it.

He always asked for 'Ho Ro, My Nut-Brown Maiden,' and gazed at Miss McKenzie from behind the piano as we sang it.

My teacher was a man, Mr Brompton. He did not seem terribly old, so was probably unfit for war service, since the only other man in the school was an ancient headmaster, Mr Wren. Mr Wren had a full teaching schedule just as Miss Samson, the headmistress, did. Mr Brompton was unapproachable, a very reserved man. He had discipline problems with some of his more unruly pupils, but not with me. After the Slogger Sloane episode I had lost any fleeting desire I ever had to fall out of line.

Mr Brompton and I once unwittingly caused one another a great deal of embarrassment. Mum and Gan had taken all of us on one of our regular visits to a Spiritualist church in Devonport, one of those where some members of the congregation were picked out to receive a message from the Other Side. As soon as we had taken our seats I saw Mr Brompton sitting beside an old lady. He jumped visibly when he turned round and saw me.

All the way through the service I was acutely conscious of him sitting two rows in front of me. While we were singing "Nearer my God to Thee" I managed to whisper to Gan, "That's my teacher over there."

"Where, where?" she whispered back and just as she finally looked in the right direction of my pointing finger, Mr Brompton cast us a surreptitious look over his shoulder. Far worse was to follow.

I had been dreading the possibility of us receiving a message, knowing Mr Brompton would be listening. As the last notes of the hymn died away, the medium stood silently for a few minutes, with closed eyes. Shuffling and scraping of chairs died away, as we all sat down in heightened anticipation.

When the woman spoke it was in a quite different voice to the one she had used to conduct the hymn singing. She had several messages. Someone called Joe was very persistent. "He wants to reassure someone who is going through a rough patch," intoned the medium's deep, man-like voice. Several people put up their hands to claim Joe.

The medium said, "I see a thick-set man with a grey beard." That cut down the claimants to an elderly couple on the front row and a young woman directly in front of us.

"He says, 'Tell Annie, better times are coming.' Does that mean anything?" The disappointed couple's hands dropped to their laps, as the young woman said eagerly, "Yes, that's his cousin on my Dad's side. He thought a lot of her."

The medium passed on several more encouraging messages from Joe, before going back to her trance-like state. She began to speak to someone we could not see.

"Yes. Yes, it's alright my dear. Yes." Silence, then she said, "Of course I will," and opened her eyes to ask, "Does anyone know a lady whose name begins with W, I am getting Wanda, or it could be Winifred, who passed to the Other Side leaving someone she was very fond of?"

In the dead silence which followed, as no-one laid claim to Wanda or Winifred, we heard the old lady's stage whisper to Mr Brompton. "It's for you, Ernest. Put your hand up. It'll be Wilma." Several people turned to look at them. I could see, even from where we sat, the dark red colour suffusing the back of Mr Brompton's neck.

The medium closed her eyes to listen intently before saying in a soothing voice, "Yes, my dear, yes". She opened them again to pronounce firmly, "It is Wilma".

There followed a very awkward exchange between the three people on this side, and Wilma on the other. The old lady, whom I guessed to be his mother, continued to press Mr Brompton in a sibilant whisper everyone could hear and Mr Brompton tried in vain to shut her up.

The medium kept reassuring Wilma. "Yes. Yes, my dear," then reproved Mr Brompton. "Was this lady your loved one?" she asked, in a deep, throbbing voice, but it was old Mrs Brompton who answered.

"Yes, yes she was. At least, that's what she always said, but I never . . . Ernest," she turned back to her son and hissed, "Tell her."

Forced into a corner, poor Mr Brompton quietly admitted, "Yes, I knew someone called Wilma."

The medium said, "Well, she wants me to tell you . . ." She listened for a moment. "She wants me to say . . . 'It was good while it lasted, my dear.' Does that mean anything to you?"

"Yes." Mr Brompton's monosyllabic reply was barely heard above his mother's sharp, "No it wasn't. She led him on something dreadful."

Mr Brompton squirmed in his seat, while several women turned indignant eyes on the truculent old lady. But the medium was equal to the occasion.

"Yes, I see trouble between two women over a man," she intoned. "But Wilma is at peace now and has this message for her loved one. 'Tell him, forgive but don't forget.' And now, we will finish our meeting with the hymn, 'O Perfect Love,'" and we all rose to our feet as the pianist thumped out the opening bars.

At eleven years old, Mr Brompton's sad little history did not make much of an impression on me. He seemed too staid to have ever had a romance. But I was deeply embarrassed at having learned his name. Ernest? How could anyone be anything other than ashamed at being called Ernest?

At school the following day I dreaded meeting him, but I need not have worried. He never said a word, did not even look at me when he passed me my exercise book. And all the time I was in his class I never told anyone that his initial E. did not stand for Edward, as most of my classmates had speculated.

In one respect, Torpoint School was no different to Millbrook. All our teachers continually impressed on us that we could all do our part to win the war.

There was the usual knitting by the girls, of balaclavas, socks and mittens, for men in the Forces. We also had frequent bazaars to raise money, for which we made a wide variety of things in our craft lessons. I learned to knit FairIsle and made gloves for all the family as well as for selling at school. We made toys, which were in very short supply, out of cardboard boxes. I made a dolls' house, with matchbox furniture, and Gan bought it for Jill, recouping the five shillings she paid for it out of the ten shillings I won for making it.

All school prizes, whether for competitions or Sports Day events, were given in National Savings, the first prize always being a fifteen shilling certificate, with ten shillings and five shillings in savings stamps for second and third prizes. I won craft prizes quite often, while Diane won sports prizes, as she developed into a good runner.

Parents also helped to stock our bazaar counters. Mum had quietly talked Gan out of making a cake. "We need all our cakes ourselves," she said diplomatically, so Gan usually sent a jar of jam.

Mum had one or two really good sellers. One was paper flowers, but her most popular contributions were her pairs of earrings made out of buttons and fuse wire. We made shopping bags from raffia and cardboard milk-bottle tops, necklaces from acorns dipped in varnish, and sea-shell-covered boxes. All our efforts were bought up by patriotic parents.

Apart from such social events, Mum and Gan at first had no other contact with any of our teachers. Mum, of course, was working. Gan did not seem to feel the same teacher-antagonism she had often shown at Millbrook. That is, until she began a long-running feud with my cookery teacher.

Mrs Proctor got off to a bad start with the first note she sent home. She asked for parents' co-operation despite food shortages, and said she would endeavour to teach her girls sensible war-time recipes which would make a useful addition to their family's diet, and might even pass on a few helpful hints to their mothers.

"What does she mean . . . 'A few helpful hints'?" Gan irritably asked me without expecting an answer. "I don't want her helpful hints! And if she thinks I'm passing over our rations for you to make a mess of, she's got another think coming." But she reluctantly gave me the ingredients I needed for my first lesson.

I got through the first few weeks of cookery without rousing too much hostility in Gan. I found I had to be careful what I said. Even telling her that Mrs Proctor said holding your hands high and letting the flour flow through them, gathering up air, was the way to get light pastry, stirred her up, but of course I should never have said it while she was in the kitchen making a corned beef and potato pie. "I've never heard such rubbish," she snapped at me. "It's cutting the pastry through that makes it light." She proceeded to demonstrate by giving the lump of dough on her board several vicious slashes with her knife.

Gan was even more incensed when I offered her one of the helpful hints Mrs Proctor had mentioned in her letter.

I had brought home a spongecake I had made, which was surprisingly well risen. Even Gan praised it and I suppose that's what really went to my head.

"Mrs Proctor says the secret is in how long you beat it," I said importantly. "She says you have to reconstitute the dried eggs not put them in dry as a lot of housewives do, just to save time, and beat them for twenty minutes before adding the flour."

Gan said rather shortly, "If she thinks beating a sponge for twenty minutes is what makes it light, she's got more time than sense. It's the self-raising flour that does it."

Once again, I could not keep my mouth shut. I blurted out, "Yes, but yours didn't rise, did it Gan. And you used self-raising flour." I was referring to the sponge she had produced the previous weekend, which had managed to sink even lower than when she had put it in the oven. We liked it. But we knew Gan was dissatisfied with it when she tried unsuccessfully to split it and in the end had to be satisfied with spreading jam over the top of it, with her cheeks flaming and a resounding "Bum" bursting from her lips. That was her worst swear word, at least the worst that we ever heard.

This time I had gone too far. I cowered back out of her reach when I saw the resentment I had unleashed. "You cheeky little madam," she shouted at me. "So that's what this Mrs Proctor is teaching you . . . to look down your nose at my cooking! I notice you didn't refuse a second slice when you were offered it. Well if that's what you think of it . . . and you can tell her from me, I've been cooking twenty years longer than she has, I have more food sense in my little finger than she has in her whole body!"

By now, everybody was alarmed. Nearly in tears I was protesting, "I didn't mean . . . I wasn't . . ." while Diane edged her chair away from mine and Jill slunk so far down in hers there was not much more than her startled blue eyes showing above the table-top. Mum tried to soothe Gan's ruffled feelings. "I'm sure Betty didn't mean to be rude, Mum," she began but Gan would not listen. She abruptly sprang up from the table, leaving us to finish our tea in an uncomfortable silence, as the remains of my sponge stuck in our throats and all but choked us.

After that, I was more careful not to pass on tips from my cookery lessons. But I still encountered difficulties. Gan continually questioned my weekly list of ingredients and often substituted her own. "What on earth does she want you to have that for?" she would demand. "Tell her, this is just as good."

If I was lucky I only had to take porridge oats instead of oatmeal, or ginger instead of cinnamon, though Mrs Proctor began to look at me askance as these substitutes happened every time. My really unlucky week was when Gan would not give me plain flour when we were making bread. "Self-raising is just as good," she insisted. Plucking up my courage I ventured, "But Mrs Proctor says we are to be sure to bring plain flour. What shall I say to her?"

"Oh for Heaven's sake!" Gan shovelled a pound of flour into a brown paper bag and thrust it at me. "Don't tell her then. She won't know the difference."

So I did not tell her. Mrs Proctor had provided us with the yeast we needed and seemed genuinely surprised when I produced the only disaster. "I don't know what's happened here, Betty," she sympathised. "Take it home by all means, but I don't think it's edible, dear."

That's what she thought. I took it home and placed it carefully on the kitchen table, though it still made an ominous thud. All Gan said, as she stared at the small, solid looking brown object was, "That'll do for your tea."

She had a struggle getting the saw-knife though it, but eventually managed to hack off some thick slices, which she covered with blackberry jam.

"Get it down you and be thankful," she ordered us. "The Germans are living on black bread, and they'd give anything even for this."

Eventually, I became so upset at never turning up at school with the right cookery ingredients, I began to lie my way through my embarrassment.

At first I only told small lies. Like, for instance, Gan could not give me any almond essence because she had just used the last drop. Or, the reason I had brought a few prunes when we had been asked to bring a spoonful of sultanas was because Gan was poorly.

Mrs Proctor asked kindly, "Is your Grandma often ill, Betty?" and I grasped eagerly at the sympathy I could see in her face.

"Oh yes," I told her. "Gan has never been the same since she lost Grandad in the First World War. So sometimes . . . she's too upset to think about food and things."

That was the start of a gradual picture I built up in Mrs Proctor's mind, of my sad, frail grandmother, often in bed, except when she was tottering around trying to find things for us, or crawling down to the shops with her stick. I must have been really good at it. It made the shock all the greater when Mrs Proctor and Gan finally met, and my fall all the harder.

CHAPTER
FOUR

"Civilians will be called upon to help by cooking and distributing food, filling craters and shell-holes, digging trenches, billeting soldiers and bombed-out neighbours."

(Sir John Anderson's speech on what to do on invasion 24/3/1942)

It wasn't too much of a surprise when Gan went off Mrs Crisp. In some ways, the two women were very much alike . . . strong and forthright, always convinced they were right and everybody else was wrong. But whereas Gan could hold her own in any slanging match, Mrs Crisp was far too superior to indulge in one. So when they went off one another they didn't so much fall out as start "keeping themselves to themselves".

It was Mrs Crisp's superiority, at first impressing Gan, which eventually began to annoy her.

"I don't mind her bragging about her daughter in the A.T.S." she grumbled. "And of course I'm sorry about John in the prisoner-of-war camp though, as I told her, at least he's safe now till the end of the war. But if she thinks I'm going to take her old buck about that doddery old husband of hers, she's got another think coming."

Mr Crisp was in the Home Guard. Quiet and inoffensive, he never laid the slightest claim to any glory. But his wife did it for him. She called on us the day we all received the latest invasion instructions, and immediately began to put Gan's back up. We were at school when she called, but we heard Gan's highly indignant version of it when Mum came home.

"You'd never believe the cheek of that woman," she began as soon as Mum had subsided on to a kitchen chair.

"What woman?" As usual, Mum was worn out.

Gan was always impatient at being questioned. "Who do you think? Madam Crisp of course! She's been here today swanking about her old man and what he'll be doing if we're invaded. I can tell you, it was all I could do not to be rude." We knew that meant she had been.

Mum picked up the cup of tea Gan had put at her elbow and gratefully sipped it. "So what's she been saying?" she asked, resigned.

"Here, read this first." Gan thrust a leaflet in front of her. "Tell me what you think of it."

Mum dutifully read it. "Well, we knew we were getting another warning," she said. "It's much the same as the last one, isn't it, except for the bit about the scorched earth policy."

"Never mind about that," Gan snapped at her. "Read the bit about the Military being in control if a town or village is cut off. What's your idea of 'Military'?"

"Why, soldiers, of course." Mum shot her a puzzled glance. "Exactly," said Gan in triumph. "Soldiers. Not Henry Crisp. Though if you believed all his wife says you'd think he was personally organising the whole of

Torpoint's civilian resistance. Why, he couldn't organise a Sunday School party, let alone one to dig trenches."

"Dig trenches?"

"That's what I'm telling you! She says his platoon has been given responsibility for organising parties of civilians to dig trenches, if the Germans invade us."

Mum said reasonably, "Well, that's quite likely, Mum. The Home Guard are being given more and more responsibilities as the real army goes to fight. Debbie was telling me her Dad's platoon has been put on night duty, manning a searchlight."

She put down her cup and cast Gan a mischievous glance. "She told me a good tale today. She reckoned one of her Dad's Home Guard mates went to a cottage late at night and talked the woman there, who was on her own, into believing he was a soldier on embarkation leave. The upshot was . . ."

Mum suddenly seemed to become aware of us three children sitting silently around the table, though it was not an unusual situation. We had long followed the Victorian maxim, instilled into us by Gan, that we should be seen but not heard.

She looked at Gan and slowly enunciated, "He asked her for a appy-h emory-m to ake-t with him, and she gave him one."

Gan was instantly diverted. "Are you telling me she didn't notice his grey hair?" she asked incredulously.

"Grey hair? Ben's as bald as a coot but Debbie says he would have had his cap on. And anyway, it was pitch black and apparently the woman had turned her light out because her blackout curtain had fallen down. So old Ben offered to help her put it back up."

Gan brought Mum's dinner from the oven, of which we'd had our share earlier. A thick piece of corned beef and carrot pie, surrounded by a generous mound of Oxo-soaked potatoes, was set on the table.

Her tone was scornful. "Well if that woman was daft enough to let a stranger into her house in the dark, and especially one in uniform, she was asking for trouble. There, get that down you."

Mum picked up her knife and fork. "That's not the end of the story," she chuckled. "Debbie's Dad called back at the cottage the following morning, after they'd finished their stint on the searchlight, to return the milk jug. He swears the woman who answered the door was sixty-five if she was a day. So that was the end of poor old Ben's glory. They all reckoned he'd been well and truly had."

At eleven years old I was still sexually ignorant. Gan's loud guffaw at Mum's tale seemed to me out of all reason. "Serve the old devil right," she chortled, then caught my puzzled stare. "Little pitchers have big ears," she hissed at me. "You and Diane, go and get washed ready for bed. And make sure you don't miss your necks."

I learned more about this latest invasion warning at Cookery School that week, because Mrs Proctor used it as a basis for a pep talk.

"It's very important that every girl should be able to cook," she earnestly told us, as we stood in a circle around her large demonstration table. I couldn't take my eyes off the pathetic little rabbit stretched out on a board in front of her.

42

"The Government has asked that, if we are invaded, women, and that includes you girls, should be prepared to cook and distribute food to others if they are in need."

Nora Staples was quick to speak up. "But not for the Germans, Miss," she said importantly. "We have to hide it from them."

"Quite true, Nora," Mrs Proctor answered gravely. "All food must be kept well out of sight of the enemy, particularly any tinned food your mothers may have saved. However, I shall be concerned this term with teaching you how to cook simple meals for your family perhaps while your mothers and older brothers and sisters are occupied in digging trenches or filling in craters and shell-holes, or any other of the jobs civilians would be expected to take over if we were invaded. So," she cast a keenly speculative glance along our solemn faces, "How many of you could skin a rabbit?"

"How many of you could skin a rabbit?"

None of us could. I knew Gan had skinned countless rabbits but I had never actually watched her. I began to feel squeamish as soon as Mrs Proctor picked up her knife. I never remembered anything she said after that. I watched her turn the rabbit over onto its back and before she had made the first incision I had keeled over on top of Nora Staples, dragging her down with me onto the hard, stone-flagged floor. The next thing I remembered was sitting on a chair with Mrs Proctor's hand on the back of my neck, firmly thrusting my head down to my knees.

I think most of the girls were quite impressed. And Mrs Proctor, good teacher that she was, got a lesson out of the situation. As soon as I felt better she gathered the class around me, instead of the rabbit, and gave us a talk on why the mere sight of blood is enough to make some people faint.

"It's because seeing blood flashes a message to your brain that something is wrong," she told us.

I think poor Nora Staples must have felt a little neglected. A short, slightly built girl, she had been floored by the tallest girl in the class. She sniffed, "I never faint, Miss. Not even when my brother got in a fight and came home with blood pouring from his . . ."

Mrs Proctor firmly interrupted. "And a good thing too, Nora. We need people who are unaffected by the sight of blood, to be our doctors and nurses." She saw Nora's triumphant glance round and added, "But remember girls, those of us who are affected are not cowards. They are simply more sensitive than others."

She was so kind, and my classmates so impressed, I didn't like to tell her that I hadn't even waited to see any blood. Just the knowledge of what she was going to do to the rabbit had been sufficient to finish me off.

Gan was in a bad mood when I got home. I could tell by the wary expressions on Diane's and Jill's faces, before she spoke a word.

"Well, what useless tips has she been passing on to you this week," she demanded. I decided not to tell her about the rabbit.

"She's been telling us how we could help if we were invaded," I said. "We'd have to cook the dinners while you were out digging trenches."

"She says I'd have to cook the dinner
while you were out digging trenches."

"Oh you would, would you? Heaven help us all."
She berated Jill, "Stop sniffing, for Heaven's sake,"
and poor Jill gave one last, desperate sniff then held
her breath until Gan had returned her attention to
me.

"So. What masterpiece is she teaching you next
week?" She held out her hand and I gave her the list of
cookery ingredients I'd been clutching.

"It's for lentil soup," I said. "Mrs Proctor says it's a
good standby in an emergency because most
housewives have the ingredients already in their
store-cupboards."

I saw Gan's expression hardening as her eye ran
down the innocuous enough list and my spirits sank.
She was going to be awkward, as she usually was, about
giving me what I had been told to bring.

"Half a pint of lentils. None of us like tomatoes, so
there's no point in taking them. Or cheese. You can
have a carrot but you're not having any of my onions,
not after I queued for half an hour yesterday for a
measly pound. And you don't need parsley. You can
take a bit of dried mint instead. Half an ounce of
marge." She made no comment but then read out,
"One dessertspoon of cornflour. Well, I haven't any.
You'll have to make do with self-raising flour."

She looked up, catching my downcast expression
before I had time to hide it, and snapped, "And you can
take that miserable look off your face. You tell your
cookery teacher from me, all you need for lentil soup is
lentils."

Of course, I didn't tell Mrs Proctor any such thing. By my next cookery lesson I had invented another sob-story.

"Gan cried when I told her I was making lentil soup," I told my teacher. "That was Grandad's favourite meal. She was really upset so I couldn't . . ." I hesitated. "I've brought what I could find."

I must have looked pathetic because Mrs Proctor said kindly, "Never mind, Betty. You've brought the main ingredient, though it's a pity you couldn't even find a scrap of cheese, dear."

I explained, "We never have any cheese. Nobody in our house likes it."

Mrs Proctor looked at me intently. "So you don't use your cheese ration? What a terrible waste."

Always anxious to please anyone who was kind to me, I eagerly offered, "If you like, I'll ask Gan to let you have it, Mrs Proctor."

Of course she accepted. I crawled home from school that afternoon, carrying a bowl of thankfully solid soup in my string bag, trying to come up with a way of asking Gan for the cheese for Mrs Proctor, which would not invite an automatic refusal. My story had become clear in my mind by the time I turned up the back street to our flat.

Gan was ready with a saucepan, into which she scraped the soup. "It looks good and thick," she approved. "It'll do nicely for your tea."

"Mrs Proctor wasn't very well today." I took off my coat, hung it on the door-peg, and resolutely closed my mind's eye to its picture of Mrs Proctor's rosy-cheeked face and well nourished body. "She isn't very strong and has to eat more cheese. Myra Simpson's mother is going to let her have their ration because they don't take it. Mrs Proctor is very grateful because that means she will get an extra six ounces a week. She only gets two ounces herself."

Gan never liked to be outdone. "Tell her she can have ours too," she said grandly. "I bet she won't say no to another ten ounces." I couldn't believe it had been so easy.

The next day, Gan's relationship with Mrs Crisp followed what was to us a very familiar pattern. She caught a glimpse of that lady passing the kitchen window, as we sat down to our midday lunch of bread and a mug of Oxo, and hissed at us, "Down on the floor, quick." It says much for her iron control over us that we were all crouched behind the table within two or three seconds, although Jill did spill her Oxo on the way down.

I began to whisper, "What . . . ?" but got no further. With a fierce "Sssshhh," Gan flopped down beside us, just as a knock came on the back door.

The awful thing was, I knew Mrs Crisp must have seen the flurry of movement through the window, as we scrambled for cover, and I had reached an age when I was capable of embarrassment. It was a feeling Gan was seldom inflicted with. When I voiced my fear, after Mrs Crisp had given up and gone away, her prompt retort was, "Serve her right. That's what she gets for staring in folks' windows."

48

CHAPTER
FIVE

"Let them talk to you of their homes and families. Remember how homesick they must be"

(Advice in a women's magazine on how to make foreign servicemen feel welcome.)

Gan was often exasperated with me, but never more so than when I began to go through what I can only describe as a "delayed action" phase. It was as though things I saw had to go through a filter in my brain, before coming back to be understood.

"Whatever's the matter with you?" she would scold me. "Talk about being slow on the uptake . . . yours never even gets started."

Once, when we were walking home from the Forum in Devonport, to catch the ferry home, I made a find. We must have walked a hundred yards past it before I realised what it was and said to Gan, "I'm sure I saw a ten shilling note back there."

She cast me an impatient glance. "Well, go and pick it up, then," she snapped and I did. I spent it on taking us all to the cinema again, five one-and-ninepennies with one-and-three left over for sweets.

Coming home on the bus from Plymouth one day, my uptake let me down again.

Plymouth was full of foreign servicemen, in addition to our own sailors. Going upstairs on the crowded bus, I had to take a seat next to a man in naval uniform, who began talking to me in heavily accented English. He told me he was Polish.

He was a very friendly man, and viewed from my eleven years, not particularly young. He said he had a daughter like me in Poland and spoke so sadly, I felt sorry for him. Young as I was, I realised he must be homesick, wanting someone to talk to.

"Is she about my age?" I asked him.

"A little girl," he said, giving my green, outgrown coat a quick look over. "She is not as big as you."

He told me about his ship. "She lies up the river, away from the bombs," and I gravely told him, "But you mustn't tell me about your ship. 'Careless Talk Costs Lives.' "

He thought that was very funny, though I was quite serious. We were frequently reminded at school that we were never to give helpful information to strangers.

His hat was on his lap and he drew my attention to it. He gave me a smiling, sideways glance. "You have seen one like this before?" he asked softly.

"Oh yes," I assured him. "Lots of them, especially in Plymouth."

He seemed surprised. "You know what it means?"

I looked at his cap band, with it's foreign inscription. "Well, no," I admitted. "I've only seen English ones before."

I heard Mum calling me from the back of the bus. "This is where I get off," I said. "It's been a pleasure," he smiled.

Mum and Gan were interested to hear what we had been talking about and I repeated our conversation as we walked down Ferry Road. "He was homesick," I told them. "He wanted to talk about his daughter in Poland. And he showed me his hat."

For once, Gan was approving. "Those men must be very lonely, poor souls. Heaven knows if they'll ever see their families again."

We were half way to the ferry before a hitherto unregistered image surfaced in my brain. Unsure, I said slowly to Mum, "I'm sure there was something under his hat he was showing me. Something pink."

Mum turned a horrified look from me to Gan. Gan's response was typically robust. "Well, what was it?" she demanded.

"I don't know." I didn't either, growing up as I had in an entirely female family. "Something he was hiding." Ignorant though I was, even I began to have uncomfortable suspicions.

There was a long silence, broken only by our hurrying footsteps down the ferry slope, before Mum said thankfully to Gan, "Well, there's one thing, he must have realised how innocent she was."

"Well there's one thing, he must have realised
how innocent she was."

"Innocent?" Gan snorted. "Daft more like. You
know, Ida, we'll have to have a talk with the girls."

So that incident led to Diane's and my first lesson in
sex. It wasn't prolonged and had no finesse. Given by
Gan in her forthright, no-nonsense way, I suspect there
was also a hint of embarrassment in her tone.

She brusquely told us, "Don't ever trust a man who
shows you something . . . down below. It means he's
sick-minded. And he could hurt you with it. Never
mind how," she forestalled any question before Diane
or I could frame one. "Just take my word for it. And
don't," with a grim glance at me, "stop to bandy words.
Just get out of his way as quick as you can."

As a warning, we took it seriously enough. But as a
lesson in biology we learned nothing. For ages
afterwards I was convinced that a man could squirt out
a poisonous venom from his trousers, just like a snake.

Despite Gan's strong common sense, she had a gullible side to her character in anything concerning clairvoyance. In addition to regular sorties to Spiritualists in Devonport and Plymouth, and the dramatic events she frequently saw in the tea-leaves, or her crystal ball, Gan began seeing spirits herself. As though that didn't satisfy her, she continually put pressure on us all, except Jill who was too young, to see what she saw.

Mum seemed to get out of it. "Your mother already has the special gift of being able to write to Sir Percy," Gan gravely told us. "So it's up to you two. Close your eyes and you will see them." She said it in such a forceful way, Diane and I were afraid to confess that we couldn't.

So we saw what she wanted us to see. Ethereal figures of Scarlet-Pimpernel-type men and women wearing Regency dress, mingled with uniformed young men of our own generation, new recruits to Sir Percy's League. From nationally famous air-aces like Paddy Finucane, who had been posted missing, to local sailors who had gone down with their ships, Gan saw them all and convinced us we did too.

Of course, it was just mind's eye pictures we saw, but to me especially they began to seem very real. I could see Gan's spirits so clearly, I never felt that I was lying as I vividly described those people who were not there. It still amazes me, after all these years, that Gan, who had caught me out in so many tall stories, really did believe I was seeing things.

After a long session of these home séances in 1942, Gan suddenly lost her enthusiasm for them. One day, when Mum came home, Gan said with tears in her eyes, "Did you hear the news? We've lost . . . " She named a then famous airman.

"He's been reported missing," Mum said. "There's still hope."

"No, he's gone." Gan's tone was sad but quite emphatic. "I've seen him."

Then, a few days later, the missing airman was reported as being a prisoner-of-war. Gan was in no way put out of countenance. "Thank the Lord," she said fervently. "Mind you, he must have been very close to death for me to have seen him." But after that, she left the business of seeing spirits to the Plymouth mediums, and went back to her tea-leaves.

With a recently drained tea-cup in her hand, and an attentive audience, Gan was in her element. She was used to her skill commanding respect from her neighbours. So it was with the complacency of knowing she was conferring favour, that she invited Mrs Shipley down for a reading.

We had come home from school to find Mrs Shipley already installed at the kitchen table. She always spoke kindly to us. "Hullo, girls," she smiled. "Your Gran and I are just going to see what the future has in store for us." She gave us a broad wink which, always sensitive to Gan's moods, I knew at once had annoyed her.

"You two, take Jill out in the yard to play," she sharply ordered us. "I'll tell you when it's time to come in." She held out her hand towards her neighbour. "Now let's see what's in your cup."

I dawdled as much as I dared, helping Diane to look for our skipping ropes, then winding Jill into a thick wool scarf against the cool Spring air. Gan's tea-leaves readings always fascinated me. Unable myself to see anything significant in the dregs of leaves from the cup's rim to its base, the amount depending on how near the bottom of the teapot had been reached, I was deeply impressed by Gan's often sensational interpretations.

I heard Gan solemnly pronounce, "I see trouble in the tea-leaves. And I mean . . . Trouble with a capital T! It's to do with a woman."

She paused. "You'll have to be careful you don't get involved in a quarrel between an older woman and someone she's interested in. Don't be drawn." I peered over her shoulder, trying to see what she was seeing, as she added, "There's a letter M next to a dog, half way down your cup. That means a friend who is not to be trusted, with the letter M in her name."

Mrs Shipley laughed. "You'd better tell me what your name is, Mrs Cooper," she joked. "Then I'll know whether it's you I have to avoid."

Jill and I both choked, and Gan's head shot round to glare at us.

"What are you trying to do, strangle the child?" she demanded and that indeed was what I had almost done, in the fluster of remembering her name was Mabel.

She unwound Jill and flung the scarf at me. "You don't need scarves, you'll get plenty warm enough if you skip hard. Now, off with you."

As we were going out of the kitchen door she continued, "As I was saying, Mrs Shipley, watch out for a false friend, especially if she's a blonde." Gan's hair was iron grey.

I heard Mrs Shipley's infectious giggle as I was quietly closing the door behind us. "Well, that applies to half the Make-do-and-Mend Circle, Mrs Cooper. Have another look and see if you can tell if she's bottle or bona-fide." I began to feel apprehensive for her as I followed Diane and Jill down the yard. She was taking Gan's tea-leaves altogether too lightly.

For the next twenty minutes we skipped up and down the path, past the kitchen window. I couldn't see Gan's face, as she sat with her back to the window, but Mrs Shipley's face was clearly visible. Every time I looked in she was registering a little less bonhomie and a little more unease. Her face was so expressive, I could tell the rate of Gan's fall-out with her.

My last view of Mrs Shipley was of her on her feet, her face red and reproachful, before she made for the hall door leading to her flat.

We didn't dare go in until Gan called us. When she did, she couldn't hide her disgust of Mrs Shipley.

"That's the last time I invite her in for a reading," she fumed. "She just thought it was all one big joke. Even when I told her there was an anchor in her cup, which is a sign of hope, all she could say was, 'What a shame, I thought it would be a sailor.' Well that's it. She won't get in again."

Mrs Shipley gave no sign of wanting to. She kept out of our way for weeks after, until a surreptitious game of marbles in the backyard between Diane, me and Peter made the first crack in the ice between her and Gan.

My often slow reactions to what I saw ultimately earned me, not only Gan's, but the Gypsy's Warning. On my way out to the shops one afternoon after school, I met on the doorstep a smiling woman with a red turban round her head, and big gold rings dangling from her ears.

"Hullo, dearie," she said. "Run and tell your Mum that Rose has got some good news for her."

I did as she asked. "There's a lady outside," I told Gan. "I think she knows Mum."

Gan peered through the window but couldn't see her. "Who is she?"

"I don't know. But she's called Rose and she has a message for Mum." Gan followed me to the door, where I left her to talk to Mum's friend.

When I got home, Gan was furious with me. "Why

"There's a lady outside," I told Gan. "I think she knows Mum."

didn't you tell me it was a gypsy," she shouted. "I wouldn't have come to the door if I'd known."

"G . . . ypsy, " I stammered. "B . . . but . . ." I saw the bundle of clothes pegs lying on the kitchen table, and gulped, "I remember now, she had pegs in her basket." Red turban, golden ear-rings, a basket of pegs. Surely all that should have registered 'Gypsy' even in me!

Gan certainly thought so. I thought she was going to hit me. Before she had got out, "I'll give you pegs," I had shot round the other side of the kitchen table, out of her reach.

She drew a deep, angry breath and glared at me across the table. "Well that's it. That's the last time you get away with this silly habit of not seeing something that's right in front of your nose. We've just about had enough of it. Your mother will flatten you when she gets home."

I knew she wouldn't, but took Gan's rider more seriously. "And if she doesn't, I will." Either her threat had its effect, or I simply grew out of what must have been one irritating habit before developing another.

CHAPTER
SIX

"Wear light-coloured clothes.
Not only will they have a cheering effect —
they will minimise the danger of you
being run over in the blackout."

(Advice in a women's wartime magazine.)

One Sunday afternoon, Mum went down to meet the ferry and brought home a gentleman-friend for tea.

We three children had known nothing of his existence until the morning of his visit, when Mum and Gan gave us the few details they felt necessary.

Soft colour glowed in Mum's cheeks as she told us, "His name is Sam," while Gan added, "But you must call him Mr Wetherby, unless he says otherwise."

The excitement amongst us children was tremendous. Not only a visitor for tea, which was rare enough, but a man, the first to enter our exclusively female circle.

While Diane and I were still taking it in, Jill piped up, "What will we be having for tea?" But Gan always hated to be questioned. "Never you mind," she admonished Jill. "Mr Wetherby will be glad to take pot luck." I saw a shade of alarm cross Mum's face but couldn't wait to burst out with my own thrilled question.

Diane asked anxiously, "Are we going to use the best plates, Mum?" She meant the half dozen or so uncracked ones.

"Is he paying you his addresses, Mum?" I was half way through Georgette Heyer's *Regency Buck*, and knew all about the formal language of courtship.

Before Mum could answer, Gan snapped at me, "No, he isn't. I don't know where you get these daft ideas from," though she must have known I got them from books. "He is your Mother's gentleman-friend, that's all there is to it."

Crushed into a bashful silence I heard Diane anxiously ask, "Are we going to use the best plates, Mum?" She meant the half dozen or so uncracked ones. Even at ten years old, Diane had a sense of what was due to guests.

Unfortunately, Gan hadn't. There was often a strangely perverted streak of snobbery in her attitude to visitors, rare though they were. It was as though she must force people to accept her on her own terms, and if those terms were a little less than elegant, then hard luck.

We all remembered the time when Mrs Timble, our neighbour in Millbrook came to tea, and Gan had spread the table with newspapers, despite having several perfectly good tablecloths. And the soldiers from the searchlight lorry, which had got stuck in the narrow road outside our house. She had invited them in, laid cake and tea in front of them, and invited them to "bog in". Heaven knows where she got that expression from, but she used it more than once to mortify us.

"No, we aren't," Gan retorted, once more putting her oar in before Mum could open her mouth. "Anyone would think it was the king who was coming to tea."

Mum asked hesitantly, "Shall I get out the check tablecloth, Mum?", obviously remembering the newspaper episode, and Gan instantly bridled.

"For Heaven's sake, Ida. Surely he can take us as he finds us?" It had taken her less than five minutes to put a damper on our high spirits. Mum tightened her lips and said no more.

We silently watched Gan peeling potatoes for our Sunday dinner, to a truculent accompaniment of, "Take me over there, drop me anywhere, Liverpool, Leeds and Birmingham, well I don't care". Then, our guardian angel intervened.

Mum, who was scraping carrots, suddenly put down her knife and with a serious expression on her face, went to the sideboard and picked up a pad and pencil.

We all knew what to expect. Gan stopped singing and watched Mum with as much awed respect as the rest of us.

Sir Percy seemed quite agitated. Mum's pencil darted across her pad, in a quick, indecipherable scrawl to the right and with long, heavy sweeps to the left. Between them, they wrote a whole pageful before Mum looked up and spoke very gently to Gan.

"Sir Percy says, put on a little style for your visitor, m'dear. Show the young man what real hospitality is." She glanced down at her pad and read out, "He says, 'you must often be tired, m'dear, and not feel like making an effort. But you owe it to yourself, and to others in these dark times, to demonstrate your flair for making a good show. Don't forget, members of the League are an inspiration to others.'"

And that did it. We had the green and white check tablecloth, the un-cracked, willow-pattern plates, and the table sumptuously laid with Gan's specially selected ginger cookies (I mean the unburnt ones), her thinnest cut corned beef and polony sandwiches, and an orange jelly lavishly decorated with a small tin of mandarins she had been hoarding since Christmas.

Sam wasn't a bit like I had imagined. For some reason I had anticipated a tall, dark man, not unlike the hero in the book I was reading. Sam was certainly dark, with straight, well-Brylcreemed hair, but there any resemblance to Georgette Heyer's dashing hero ended. Sam was short, a heavily built man not quite as tall as Mum. All my romantic notions plummeted.

Gan was all graciousness, as she could be when she wished. "Come in, Sam," she heartily invited him. "It's nice to meet you. I hope you've brought a good appetite with you."

It was heavy going over the tea-table, despite everyone doing justice to Gan's culinary efforts. None of us had the gift of small-talk except her, and even she had difficulty carrying on a spirited conversation with five tongue-tied individuals. Sam was as shy as we were, and Mum was always socially inhibited in Gan's presence. It was a relief to everyone when she and Sam went out for a walk.

We didn't see a great deal of Sam after that, and when we did he never had much to say. But Mum said she liked him, and we all benefited by his generosity. He lived on a farm and always brought a welcome gift when he called for Mum, a jar of cream or two or three eggs and quite often, a rabbit.

Gan wasn't so approving when Sam bought Mum a new dress.

"It's not right letting a man buy you clothes," she said, her expression severe. "It gives them ideas."

Mum flushed. "Oh Mum . . . Sam isn't like that. He just wanted me to have the benefit of some of his coupons."

"Hmph!" Gan gave Mum's new pale yellow dress a disparaging glance. "Anyway, why couldn't he have chosen brown, instead of that light colour. It'll show the dirt every time you wear it!"

Mum said, incomprehensibly, but with spirit, "So you'd rather I got run over just as long as my clothes don't show the dirt!" and earned herself an exasperated snort from Gan. (See chapter heading.)

Another of Mum's friends brought a little excitement into our lives. Debbie, who worked with her in the Dockyard, invited us all to a Beetle Drive at her home, profits to be given to Warships Week funds. It was to be held on a Saturday afternoon, to avoid the blackout.

Debbie was a smartly dressed, vivacious little blonde woman. There was a lovely, cheerful atmosphere in her small terraced house, which was full of excited people chattering away so avidly no one noticed how little we had to say. There were several small children there, so Jill was put to play with them, while Mum and Gan, Diane and I joined the Beetle tables.

Halfway through the afternoon, everything stopped for refreshments. Guests had been asked to bring a small contribution, such as one or two spoonfuls of tea, or a few biscuits or cakes. We saw Gan's offering, half a dozen nicely substantial Carrot Cookies on a big tray, flanked by a mass of smaller, lighter-coloured cakes on one side, and some flat, golden-baked biscuits on the other.

Debbie waited until they were all gone before she laughingly told us, "You'll never believe it, girls, but all of those were Carrot Cookies. It just goes to show, never mind the ingredients, it's all up to the cook."

Instinctively, my eyes searched out Gan's face. There was a flush in her cheeks, which could have been caused either by her proneness to see a slight in any reference to her cooking, however oblique, or from the mouthful of hot tea she had just gulped down.

One seam had gone off-course,
just past Debbie's left knee.

Debbie drew Mum's attention to her tan-painted legs, turning round to show her the backs. "What do you think, Ida? Do you reckon someone's made a good job of my seams?" She pulled up her skirt to display the pencilled lines up her legs, with a broad wink at Mum over her shoulder.

One seam had gone off-course, just past Debbie's left knee, but Mum loyally assured her friend, "Dead on, Debbie. You must know someone with a steady hand."

Debbie chuckled. "Well, Jack Dolon did it and I must say, his hand was steadier than I had expected."

We went on drawing legs and heads on beetles until five o'clock, when Debbie handed out the prizes. One woman won a lemon but she seemed envious of another whose prize was a pound of onions. But everyone had enjoyed themselves and Debbie had collected three pounds twelve shillings for Warships Week.

Going home on the bus, from the seat behind them I could hear Mum and Gan discussing Debbie's party. Mum said, "That made a nice change, Mum, didn't it?"

"Yes," agreed Gan. "It certainly did."

"I thought she put on a marvellous show, considering she's on her own."

"You're right there. She seems to manage very well without her husband."

There was a little pause before Mum said reproachfully, "You can't blame her for making the best of things, Mum. She's not the sort of girl to sit and mope."

"No one expects her to. But I think she could be a little less blatant about her men-friends, while her husband's away risking his life at sea."

Mum was indignant. "Men-friends? If you mean Jack Dolon, he's harmless. He's one of the overseers and he flirts with all the girls. It doesn't mean a thing."

Gan was sarcastic. "Well, I wasn't born yesterday, Ida, even if you were. You saw where that stocking line was crooked."

"B . . . but what's that got to do with anything?" Mum seemed genuinely bewildered. Diane and I exchanged glances over Jill's placidly drooping head. We were becoming intrigued.

"You saw where it was? Well, tell me this, why did his hand jerk after her knee?"

After a moment of shocked silence, Mum sprang to her friend's defence. "That's not fair," she protested. "Debbie was quite open about Jack Dolon. She obviously had nothing to hide. Anyway, if that's what you think about her, we won't go to her next Beetle Drive."

"Oh, for heaven's sake." As though conscious she had raised her voice, Gan shot a suspicious glance over her shoulder at us. With lightning reaction, we both bent to fuss over Jill.

Gan hissed at Mum, "I'm not saying it wasn't a good party. It was. I'm just warning you . . . it's my belief that young woman's no better than she should be. And if her husband gets wind of Jack Dolon when he comes home . . . there'll be trouble in the Amen Corner!" And with that final, not-to-be-argued-with pronouncement, both she and Mum relapsed into a huffy silence.

But if Gan could adopt a moralistic attitude over Mum's friends, she chose her own with remarkable liberalism.

She made a friend of a down-and-out woman we met one day, as we were collecting combustibles along the Tamar shoreline. Old Margy, as we later found, lived rough in the hedgerows of the narrow lanes climbing out of Torpoint. She was a very brown, wrinkled woman, though it was difficult to tell her age. She always wore long clothes, down to her ankles, though whether this was for extra warmth, or because they had previously had much taller owners, we didn't know. She looked fit and strong, and it was a surprisingly deep, hearty voice which came from her small body.

The first time we saw her, she was walking slowly along the shingle ahead of us, frequently stopping to examine some object at her feet. She had a huge hessian sack across her back, into which she stuffed her finds.

Diane and I and, I suspect, Mum, began to feel embarrassed as we caught up with her, seemingly on the same scavenging errand as she was. But Gan would not let us dawdle back.

"What does it matter?" she demanded. "And anyway, it's everybody's duty to save as much fuel as they can. We're being patriotic."

But old Margy was not after the same things as we were. In response to Gan's jocular greeting, and her comment that there was plenty of wood and cork for all of us, Margy boomed, "Bless you, me 'andsome, I'm not after firewood. I'm not allowed to light a fire in case them Germans see it and drop their bombs on Torpoint. Mind you, I reckon I could have set the whole hedge on fire when the oil tanks was caught last year, and no-one would have noticed it."

We left Gan to chat with her and walked on to fill our own bags. When Gan eventually rejoined us, she was full of compassion for the old woman.

"I don't know how that poor soul survived, sleeping out last winter. Fancy, she can't even light a fire, she has to rely on folk giving her a hot drink."

Mum asked, "What's she collecting, if it isn't for a fire?"

"Things to make her hedge more comfortable," answered Gan. "An old bit of carpet, which will have to dry out first, a fish-box for a seat, some rope she says will do to tie a branch of hawthorn out of her way. Things like that."

Gan paused, before a new note of defiance hardened her voice. "Well, I've told her she's to call in for a cup of tea, any time she's passing the end of our road."

None of us said anything. I'm afraid we all lacked Gan's charity. I remember thinking that, with a bit of luck, we'd be at school, and I expect Mum had the same cowardly hope of being out when old Margy called.

CHAPTER
SEVEN

"Civilians to stand firm . . . to try to overcome stray enemy marauders, hide food, but not to attack enemy military formations without orders."

(Sir John Anderson's speech on invasion — 24/3/1942.)

Sitting in the kitchen one Saturday morning, finishing off some brittle, inadequately scraped toast which Gan had firmly declared could not be wasted, "And anyway, a bit of charcoal is good for your teeth," we could see her talking to Mrs Crisp over the garden fence.

We were all pleasantly surprised. Several weeks had elapsed since Gan and Mrs Crisp had begun to politely ignore one another. And with Gan's demand for absolute loyalty from us we had, as always, shared the icy atmosphere which descended whenever they met.

We could hear the pleasant murmur of animated conversation. Then, at first imperceptibly, Gan's voice began to get louder, until we were able to pick out the odd word. "Fifth Columnists", we heard and "puggled", which was slightly alarming because it was a word she used in place of "daft".

But it was when "You needn't worry, I shan't pry," penetrated the tightly closed door and window, that our raised spirits plummeted. The truce had lasted for less than ten minutes.

Gan came in, her exasperation out-bursting before she had even closed the door. "Well, that explains why That Woman condescended to speak to me! All she wanted to do was swank about knowing something hush-hush, that she can't talk about. I ask you . . . can you imagine that decrepit old man of hers being involved in anything hush-hush? All he's doing is playing at soldiers."

"Do you mean something to do with the Home Guard?" Mum asked. "Well, they are under Army discipline. Debbie was telling me two men in her Dad's platoon have just been court-martialled."

Gan was startled. "Whatever for?"

"They were supposed to be on sentry duty, but nipped off to the canteen for a cup of tea. And one of them had left his rifle behind."

"Serve them right," Gan said indignantly. "Much good they'd have been if the Germans had landed." But she still refused to accept that poor Mr Crisp could be doing anything vital to the War Effort.

"He'd never be able to stand on sentry duty with his feet. I know for a fact he's got two bunions the size of sparrow eggs."

71

"And as for Henry Crisp . . . he'd never be able to stand on sentry duty with his feet. I know for a fact he's got two bunions the size of sparrow eggs."

A few days later, Mrs Shipley came to our kitchen door with an *Evening Herald*. "I've just been talking to Mrs Crisp," she said. "Have you seen this, Ida?" She waved the paper in front of Mum, who knew better than to accept it before Gan. "Invasion of Cornwall Practice over the Weekend," Gan read. "So that's what her hubby was up to."

"Yes, poor Mr Crisp," Mrs Shipley giggled. "He ended up being a casualty, though it was supposed to be the Boy Scouts."

"What happened?" Gan was so intrigued, she forgot that Diane and I were supposed to be following Jill to bed. We sank into our chairs, trying not to be noticed.

"It seems he was hiding behind a garden hedge when this woman comes out and tells him to b . . . off, or she'd clout him with a saucepan. He tried to tell her he was one of the defenders, but she wouldn't listen . . . everybody had been warned about the exercise by loud-hailer vans and told to stay indoors. This woman insisted she would do the same to any real Germans who hid in her garden. So when she went back inside and came rushing out with a frying pan which was still smoking, he ran. He fell over a tree stump and twisted his ankle and had to be carried off to the Red Cross post. He says they were glad to see him . . . there hadn't been enough Boy Scouts to go round."

Gan was more than ready for a gossip. "Come in and have a cup of tea," she invited. "Ida, go and put the kettle on. You girls, off to bed."

In some perverse way, Mr Crisp's misfortune reconciled Gan to Mrs Crisp. Diane and I came home from school the following afternoon to find them both ensconced in the kitchen over a cup of tea and a slice of Gan's latest delicacy, Apricot Bake . . . sliced carrots set in orange jelly, on a thick pastry base.

"He did his bit, just as much as the others," Gan was assuring her neighbour. "It's men like him we are relying on." Diane and I exchanged startled glances.

Mrs Crisp put down her slice of Apricot Bake to earnestly nod her head. "That's just what I said, Mrs Cooper. Henry was very upset. He'd been quite looking forward to going into action. The enemy were trying to form a bridgehead, you know, cutting Cornwall off from the rest of England. Henry should have been playing a vital role. Instead, he ended up on a stretcher between two damaged Boy Scouts. But I told him, I said, it's a good job it was only a practice, at least you'll be prepared for the real thing."

"Yes. Well . . . Betty, before you take your coat off, can you go down to the shop and get me some potatoes." Gan got up, to find me some money and a bag.

Mrs Crisp was still talking. "Henry really feels his responsibilities you know, Mrs Cooper. Did you hear the latest? If we are invaded, civilians are allowed to attack stray Germans, but not military formations without orders from the Military or their representatives. That's the Home Guard, of course."

When I came back with the potatoes, Mrs Crisp had left. I wondered if she and Gan were still friends. Diane and Jill seemed cheerful enough, playing dominoes on the kitchen table, which was a hopeful sign.

I said, tentatively, "Mrs Crisp seemed upset about her husband, didn't she?"

Gan snorted. "Upset, my foot. She was back to all her old buck. It was all I could do not to tell her what I thought . . . that I would not have had so much to say if I'd had a husband who tripped over a tree root when he was supposed to be saving Cornwall."

Gan's scope for rows with neighbours was more limited in Torpoint than it had been in Millbrook. Torpoint was a small town which had grown around its ferry crossing to Devonport. It had a fairly mobile population, very different to Millbrook, which was a tightly knit, isolated village where everyone knew everyone else. After being used to having a number of neighbours with whom she could fall out, she was now reduced to two. So she took to falling out with people at second hand.

Mrs Proctor was her main, once removed, object for scorn. If only I'd had enough sense not to pass on Mrs Proctor's original helpful hints, I could have had a much happier time at cookery school. As it was, Gan developed such an aversion to my unsuspecting teacher, she never stopped being awkward about the cookery ingredients she gave me to take to school.

Mr Crisp was her other pet hate, though she hardly exchanged more than a dozen or so words with him. It was the words she exchanged with his wife which scuppered poor Mr Crisp.

Then Gan found another target at whom to aim her venom, in Sam's mother. One Sunday, when Sam had been for tea, Mum returned after walking to the ferry with him, to find Gan poring over his empty tea-cup.

"I think you should look at this, Ida," Gan said, her tone portentous.

Mum obediently stared at the mass of tea-leaves inside the cup. "Can you see the two knives crossed? That means trouble between two women. If you ask me, your Sam is a darn sight too fond of his mother."

"For Heaven's sake," Mum protested. "Just because he was telling us how she burnt her hand picking up shrapnel."

"*And* how she wouldn't go to the doctor with it, and she doesn't want him to worry about her. We all know what that means."

Mum stared. "What?"

"It means that his mother will always dominate him. She's got a hold over him by pretending she doesn't want to be a burden."

Mum's voice quivered in her indignation. "She's not like that. She's a very gentle, unassuming woman. She's always very nice to me."

Gan shrugged. "Well, don't say I didn't warn you. I tell you, there's trouble in that cup, if ever I saw it."

That was the beginning of a vendetta against Sam's mother which inevitably, in time, extended to Sam.

But though Gan's quarrels upset all of us, her friendships could be equally uncomfortable. She not only refused to ignore anyone she termed 'down on their luck'. She positively encouraged them.

In response to Gan's warm invitation, old Margy called one Sunday morning. Rain was pelting down, lashed against the kitchen window by a boisterous South-Westerly gale. Gan answered the door, to usher in a bent, bedraggled figure. Wet grey hair was plastered over Margy's forehead, where it had straggled out from under her headscarf, and rain dripped from the end of her nose.

"Look who it is," Gan said heartily and quite unnecessarily. We all watched, fascinated, as Margy squelched her way in.

"Well, I've taken you up on your offer, me lover." Margy's voice seemed to well up from her soddened boots. "If ever I could do with a cup of tea, it's now."

"Of course you can have a cup of tea," Gan said. "Jill, move out of the way. Let Margy get to the fire."

"Bless you, little maid. You stay where you are. There's room for both of us." Poor Jill, who would have obeyed Gan with the alacrity with which we all jumped to her commands didn't know what to do. Margy solved her dilemma by stretching forth a skinny hand from beneath her dark green cape, to draw Jill back to the fire.

As with any visitor, Gan dominated the conversation, while the rest of us hovered silently in the background. "Ida, get the milk," Gan ordered, while she busied herself with the teapot. "You must be soaked to the skin," she commiserated with Margy.

Margy pressed herself up against the fireguard, delicately moving out of her way the thick brown stockings and fleecy bloomers which had been hung there to dry. She spread out her long navy-blue skirt with a satisfied sigh. Her spirit was undampened, unlike her clothes.

"Don't you fret, me dear," she cheerfully told Gan. "The rain never gets through all me layers. I be as dry as a bone under me knickers." Diane and I, little prudes that we were, exchanged shocked glances.

Steam began to rise from Margy's clothes. Then we began to smell her. At first, it was the familiar smell of wet clothes drying in front of the fire. An additional whiff of scorching became apparent but that too, was well known to us. More than one of our sheets and pillow-cases carried dark brown singe marks.

"Are you sure you're not burning?" Gan asked, as she took Margy a cup of tea. Margy turned to accept it, blissfully presenting her rear to the heat of the fire. "Don't care if I am," she cackled. "I'm not wearing me best coat."

Almost imperceptibly, another odour crept in with the familiar ones, one I did not recognise. It was a stale musty smell which gradually overpowered the others. It nearly overpowered us too. Little though she was, Margy's presence took over our kitchen.

I think even Gan must have realised the room would be the better for having a few less bodies in it. Luckily, the rain had eased off and she sent Diane and me to the post-box with a letter.

When we returned home, Margy had gone and the kitchen door was wide open, despite the still blustery wind. We could tell Mum and Gan had had a few words. Gan's face was angrily flushed and Mum was shepherding Jill to the bedroom, her lips compressed.

As Jill passed Diane and me, we wrinkled our noses. "There's a funny sm . . ." Diane began, but for once, it was Mum who cut her short.

"That's enough," she snapped. "Don't let me hear another word."

We got several more visits from Margy, but only one when we were all at home, when she made less impression on us for not being wet. More memorable was the day we were waiting with a line of people for the ferry, and Margy came down the slope and loudly hailed us.

She was wearing a man's dark grey overcoat. It must have belonged to a big man because it covered most of her wellington boots and only the tips of three grimy fingers emerged from each turned-up sleeve. And she was obviously well-layered beneath the heavy coat, against the biting sea-wind. Shiny brass buttons strained against frayed button-holes, the top one hanging off by a thread to reveal the folded edge of the newspaper insulating her chest.

Her clothing might be unconventional, but Margy always seemed cheerful. She seemed not to notice the sideways stares of people in the ferry queue, the perceptible drawing back of the more fastidious of them as she marched past them to where we were standing.

Mum, Diane and I were so lacking in any social confidence, we would have crawled into a crack in the concrete beneath our feet, had it been possible. Even Jill looked round askance, at the sound of Margy's clearly audible, "How-de-do, Mrs Cooper. Haven't seen you and your maids along the beach lately."

But Gan was made of sterner stuff. She turned to face Margy, colour and head high, her voice loudly genial. "How are you?" she smiled. "No, we haven't been along the beach for ages. It's been too cold. Well," she gave the old woman a quizzical look-over, "you look well wrapped up today."

Margy cackled. "I be wrapped up like a bag o' fish an' chips," she admitted. "And you take it from me, it's true what they say ... there's nothing to beat ol' newspapers for keeping out the cold."

They talked for a minute or two, though it seemed never-ending to the less stout-hearted members of

"I be wrapped up like a bag o' fish an' chips," she cackled.

Gan's family. I kept my eyes on the too slowly approaching ferry, painfully conscious of the attention we were drawing from the silent queue behind us.

Thankfully, I heard the two women begin their loud goodbyes, as Margy prepared to continue her reconnaissance along the foreshore and Gan began to shuffle forward with us as the ferry clanged in on its heavy chains. Gan gave Margy a small packet of Kensitas cigarettes, which had "And Four for a Friend" on it.

"Is that right, am I your friend?" Margy asked, and Gan stoutly assured her, "Of course you are."

I suppose such a friendship, sustained as it was mainly by Gan's bravado, was bound to come to an end one day. When Mum came home one Friday night, she was greeted with a cup of tea and a bitter, "Well, that's it. That's the last time I give that woman anything."

Usually apprehensive when Gan fell out with her neighbours, this time we all stared at her hopefully.

"Do you know what old Margy had the nerve to do? She had the bare-faced cheek to cock her nose up at that old red coat of yours." Gan, fuming, stopped to gulp a few hasty mouthfuls of her own scalding tea.

Mum was disbelieving. "Do you mean she didn't want it?"

"Oh she wanted it alright. But not to wear in public. She reckoned it would come in handy to wrap round herself to sleep. I mean, why on earth doesn't she sleep in the scruffy old man's coat she wears? Anyone would have thought she'd be glad of a decent coat instead of that, but oh no. When I think of what else I could have

80

done with it. I told her, if that's all she wanted it for, I'd just as soon keep it to make a rag rug."

She swallowed the rest of her tea, then got up to fetch Mum's dinner, always ready the instant she came through the door. Lids clashed on saucepans, then were thumped down. Gan slapped food on a plate, still deeply rattled.

"Well I told her what I thought of her and she went away with a flea in her ear. I don't think we'll be seeing her again."

We did, but only when our paths crossed on public byways. And Margy's pride must have been as outraged as Gan's, for there was no more jovial chat between them; only a stiff-necked passing, as though they had never met.

But if we thought that was the end of Gan's proclivity for collecting lame ducks, we were mistaken. The next one was Emmy, a large, child-like woman, who was often to be met ambling down the High Street. Emmy's eccentric behaviour was accepted with tolerance in her own community. She usually took no notice of people she did not know, but this stopped applying to us when Gan made a point of stopping to chat to her one day and told her my name and that of Diane. After that, Emmy bawled greetings to us, often the length of the street, whenever we met. Without a shred of Gan's self-confidence, we tried to avoid her, nipping down a back street if we saw her first.

Gan was angry when she found out. "You're not fit to be in the League," she rebuked us. "Sir Percy will be heartily ashamed of you."

So it was a straight choice between facing Emmy's uninhibited hollering and upsetting Sir Percy. I'm afraid, when we had any choice, Sir Percy lost.

CHAPTER
EIGHT

"Did you realise . . . eight old Christmas cards will provide our commandos with a demolition carton to contain 1¼lbs of TNT?"

(Ministry of Supply appeal for salvage)

I had not been long in Mr Brompton's class, before I was moved up into Miss Samson's. She was a strong disciplinarian, but also had a sense of humour, which she shared in more relaxed situations.

I benefited in her class for being one of the half dozen or so children whom she trusted to work unsupervised. So I was allowed to spend many an afternoon in the school library, losing myself in its surprisingly wide range of books. To be given absolute freedom of choice was intoxicating but on the whole I chose well. *Last Days of Pompeii* was a mistake; I never got through it. But I avidly read most of Dickens's books there.

Miss Samson was normally a calm, well-balanced teacher, always in control even when she was angry. But just once, I saw her completely lose her temper, frightening us all out of our wits.

There were several unruly boys in the class, whom she competently ruled with a rod of iron. One day, Billy

She charged down the aisle between the desks,
to where Billy sat in temporary paralysis.

Mundy swore at her. We had no time for more than a split second of shock, before Miss Samson erupted.

She charged down the aisle between the desks, her long cardigan flapping across her outraged bosom, to where Billy sat in temporary paralysis. Before she reached him he had recovered, to spring to his feet and make a mad dash for the door. On the way there he knocked over a paraffin heater, causing a gasp of consternation from the children sitting near it.

Miss Samson's stride barely faltered. She snatched up the heater as she passed, setting it upright, headed Billy off and finally cornered him behind the blackboard. As she dragged him out by his collar she looked at us, rooted in our seats, and ordered us, "Fold your hands in your laps and don't move or talk until I come back. I have something to see to." We did not dare to do anything other, except to cast horrified glances at one another. What was she going to do to Billy?

We could hear when she was on her way back, as the sound of Billy's howls grew louder. Miss Samson strode in, red-faced and breathing heavily, pushing a crying and very wet Billy in front of her. "Go and sit down," she told him and Billy crept to his seat without a word.

Miss Samson looked sternly at our stupefied faces. "Billy has had his mouth washed out with soap and water," she said grimly. "And that's what will happen to anyone else who swears at me. Now, get out your geography books and find Africa."

Gan was full of approval when I told her and an impressed Diane and Jill about Billy's punishment. On that incident alone she formed a continuing favourable impression of Miss Samson, though it slipped a bit when I won a prize for the best imaginative writing in the class. "You can tell her from me, she must be off her head to give you a prize for your imagination," she snapped.

I was going through another awkward phase, one which annoyed the whole family this time, not just Gan.

It started with my fear of the dark. There was a tree outside the bedroom window, one of its branches sometimes giving the window a gentle tap. I lay in bed and watched it, knowing it was just a tree but seeing fearsome shapes in its moving branches. Night after night I lay watching it, unable to sleep, until Gan found out.

She resorted to a familiar ploy, to stiffen my sagging backbone. After firmly telling me it was all in my imagination she added, "And anyway, what will Sir Percy think of you? You close your eyes and think of the League and stop being so mardy." So I did, but no sooner had this particular fear fizzled out than I developed another.

I began to have the odd nightmare. After listening to Mrs Crisp talking to Gan about the time a bomb just missed Torpoint Ferry, landing instead on the police station near the ferry ramp, I woke that night in a cold sweat. I had dreamt I was on the ferry when its chains snapped and it floated out to sea, waking everyone with my cries, "I can't swim! I can't swim!"

Gan blamed the jacket potato I had eaten for supper, though when I frightened Diane another night, hissing in her ear, "It's coming," before grabbing her by the neck to hurry her away from whatever it was, I had only had a jam sandwich.

Listening to *Appointment with Fear* on the wireless brought on another nightmare. It had been a story of a young couple who got lost in a London fog, and they knocked on the door of an isolated house for shelter. The owner unfortunately turned out to be a psychopath, who fastened the young man onto a table and said when the clock struck twelve, he was going to kill him.

The girl escaped, found a policeman, but couldn't find her way back to the house. It ended with the clock beginning to strike twelve. That night, I crept out of bed in my sleep, feeling my way round the dark room until I gave Mum an awful shock by feeling for her face, and got one myself waking up to her shriek.

Gan threatened not to let me listen to any more of Valentine Dyall's *Man in Black* stories, but didn't want to disappoint Diane, who could enjoy them without any after effects. So I was given another chance.

Unluckily, the next one was even worse. There was this dentist, who carried out an experiment on a patient which involved planting new teeth into his gums and securing them there by manipulating nerves.

When the man came round from the anaesthetic he was in agony, but the dentist would not help. He said the operation had been at the patient's own risk. By this time I had begun to feel queasy, but managed to hide it from Gan's sharp glances. The story went on to several months later. The dentist prepared for his last patient of the day, sending his receptionist home as it was only for an examination. The patient was the man he had hurt so much, who clamped the dentist in the chair and told him he was going to pull out all his teeth, slowly, one by one . . . I did not hear any more because I fainted.

Everyone was fed up with me, because they missed the end of the story. And Diane was particularly incensed when Gan announced, as I was recovering sitting with my head between my knees, "Well, that's it! That's the last time either of you listen to *Appointment with Fear.* "

Ignoring Diane's anguished "Aaaahhh," she went to the sideboard and came back with a medicine bottle and a spoon. My heart sank as I recognised her remedy for all ills. "Here! A good dose of Ippycak is what you want, then off to bed. And if you dare to have a nightmare tonight, young woman, I'll wring your neck."

Though we were denied any more *Appointments with Fear*, we still listened to a great deal of radio. We enjoyed the childrens's programmes, Uncle Mac and Romany, and the popular *ITMA* and Bebe Daniels' and Ben Lyon's show. I can remember a time when all five of us were plunged into depression at having to miss an episode of a thriller because we could not afford a new battery for the wireless until Mum got her wages at the weekend.

We didn't always go to the Forum cinema in Devonport now, but began patronising the Regal in Torpoint. It was much smaller than the Forum, its seats were rather less luxurious, and films broke down more frequently, to a loud groaning, stamping and whistling from the audience until the picture was restored. But we loved going and Jill was as happy there with jam sandwiches as she was at the Forum.

Another enthusiastic visitor to the Regal was Emmy. She had her own two seats . . . one was not big enough . . . near the front, to which no-one who knew her ever disputed her right.

In one of our early visits to the Regal, stumbling along the seats in the dark after the film had started, we inadvertently sat behind Emmy. When the lights came on in the interval, she turned round and joyfully greeted us.

Gan was undoubtedly of a different species to the rest of us. Without exception, we were totally mortified, hating the attention drawn to us by Emmy's loud comments, the ominous creaking and swaying of her seats as she struggled round to face us. Gan betrayed not the slightest discomfiture. If her colour was a little high, it did not show in the cinema's artificial lights, as she calmly answered Emmy's eager questions.

"Hullo, Mrs Cooper. You here to see George? (Formby) Hullo Diane. Hullo Betty." She paused at each greeting, waiting for our response. "They've come to see George!" She stared at Mum until Gan said, "This is the girls' mother, my daughter, Emmy."

Unfortunately, Emmy misunderstood, and a noisy discussion followed, to Mum's embarrassment, before it was established that her name was Ida, not Emmy, and yes, she'd come to see George too.

My prayers for the lights to go down were eventually answered. Just before they were, Emmy noticed Jill, hiding behind her bag of sandwiches. "Give Emmy one, Jill," Gan said hastily.

Jill handed one over and Emmy immediately opened it up. "Cream cracker sandwiches," she boomed. "You like cream cracker sandwiches, Jill?" Then, to our relief, the lights were dimmed and Emmy turned away to enthusiastically join the loud cheer for George Formby, before she could tell us that she didn't.

If Gan insisted on fostering those she felt life had dealt a rotten hand, she could also put aside petty differences with neighbours when they were in trouble.

Air raids on and around Plymouth had become much less frequent and prolonged, more of the hit-and-run type. Other towns and cities became targets and one of them was Norwich, a victim of the so-called "Baedeker" raids.

The Crisp's A.T.S. daughter was stationed there. "They're in a right state," Mrs Shipley told Gan. "They've had no news of her for over a week."

"Poor souls." Gan was immediately sympathetic. "I haven't seen much of Mrs Crisp lately." Relations between her and Mrs Crisp had been of the polite but "I haven't got time to stop" order, since Mr Crisp had hobbled home the worse for wear after the Invasion Practice. "I'll nip round to see them."

Leaving me and my sisters with strict instructions about the things we were not to do while she was out, she went to the Crisps' house armed with a bottle of her blackberry wine. After staying for nearly an hour offering comfort, she came home with the empty bottle.

"Well, I think I've done them good," she announced, her face flushed with her success. "He was in a worse state than she was. I told him, 'She'll be alright. Bad news travels fast,' but it took two full glasses before he believed me."

The next morning, as Gan was scraping the last lingering lumps of porridge into our bowls, Mrs Crisp came round excitedly waving a letter.

"She's all right, Mrs Cooper. We're so relieved. And we were so grateful for the way you encouraged us yesterday. Henry said, you're just the woman he'd turn to if he had to organise any civilian working parties . . . if we're invaded, you know!"

Breakfast over, Diane and I got ready for school, picking up a bag of salvage each. We were always

90

"I told him . . . Bad news travels fast.
But it took two full glasses, before he believed me."

collecting things for recycling but this week was to be an even more intensive salvage drive.

Each class was concentrating on a particular theme. One teacher asked for old jumpers to unravel for knitting wool. Another wanted jam jars. Diane's teacher asked for worn-out stockings for making into dishcloths, and Miss Samson's request was for anything made of paper. "And not only newspapers and magazines," she urged. "Ask your mothers if they would turn out drawers and send things they no longer have any use for, such as used Christmas cards or old photos."

Gan always supported any requests for the War Effort and had given us a bag each before breakfast that morning. "Make sure you bring the bags back," she reminded us.

On inspecting her bag of stockings, Diane found they'd all had the feet cut off them. She was very put out. "What will Miss McKenzie say?" she wailed. "She didn't say she wanted them without feet."

Gan was unrelenting. "If you think you're taking our old stockings to school, with the heels full of spuds, you've got another think coming," she said flatly. "She can have them with no feet, or go without."

Examination of my own bag brought my share of consternation. Drawing out a bundle of photos I asked Gan, "Why have these got some people's faces cut out of them?"

Gan was equally short with me. "It's just one man's face, not people's."

"But why?"

"Because he was a rotter. And that's enough of your questions," she snapped.

I put the packet back in the bag. "But what shall I say if Miss Samson asks me about the holes?" Like Diane, I was a worrier.

"Oh, for Heaven's sake." Gan's patience had completely run out. "Just tell her the moths have been at them. Now, off you go, the pair of you."

Of course, we had worried unnecessarily. Miss McKenzie was very appreciative of the feetless stockings. "I'm extremely grateful to all those parents who have not only washed the stockings, but have also taken the trouble to remove the unwanted foot section." She then added hastily, "However, all stockings, in whatever condition, will make excellent dishcloths."

And since Miss Samson made no attempt to look at any of the discarded photographs, brought in by the boxful, I had no need to tell her the tale about the moths.

CHAPTER
NINE

"Pork in a Poncho" (Spam in batter)

As Christmas approached, Gan had little enthusiasm for it. "What's the use of bothering," she grumbled. "It's all very well telling us to use grated carrots and potatoes in the Christmas puddings, and dried eggs, but what about dried fruit? All I could get last week was a miserable half pound of currants. And where are we going to get a rabbit this year?"

Her depression infected us. It began to look as though that Christmas would be the worst ever, when Sir Percy came to the rescue.

While Diane and I drank our bedtime cocoa, Mum silently stood up, went to the sideboard and came back with her special pad and indelible pencil, always left there in readiness. As she sat down, her face very serious, Diane and I exchanged hopeful glances, though Gan looked as though she would be harder to cheer.

The pencil flew across Mum's pad, in the deeply indented scribble of Sir Percy's which none of us could decipher except her. She half-filled her page then looked up and solemnly addressed Gan.

"Sir Percy says, 'Never give up hope m'dear. Something will turn up, you'll see. In the meantime' ... more dynamic scribble ... 'May I suggest a small glass of your excellent blackberry wine, then wait and see what tomorrow brings.'"

It was absolutely amazing. Not the morrow, but the day after, brought a parcel from Auntie Thelma, Mum's girlhood friend who had married a steward on the *Mauretania* and had gone to live with him in America. The parcel contained tins of Spam, jars of peanut butter, eggs which had been sealed in their shells in dripping, dried bananas and apricots, and unbelievably, several pounds of Californian raisins.

The effect of that parcel was awesome. Gan's mood leapt from despair to elation. She infected us all with her high spirits as she sang all over the house. Her rendering of "We'll Meet Again" had a jauntiness Vera Lynn's never had.

The huge cracked earthenware bowl was brought into the kitchen, ingredients gathered on the table and when the thick, aromatic mixture, liberally laced with blackberry wine, was ready, Gan doled it out between a large cake tin, several pudding cloths and half a dozen screw-top jars for mincemeat.

Christmas dinner was wonderful. With Auntie Thelma's eggs eased gently from their protective coating, there was enough dripping to cook a panful of chips. Then Gan set down her crowning achievement on the table. "It's called 'Pork in a Poncho'," she told us grandly, and we all joyfully tucked into the succulent Spam in its batter coat.

Sam had spent Christmas Day with his mother. "There, I told you," Gan had scorned. "She's determined to keep him tied to her apron strings."

Her rendering of "We'll Meet Again"
had a jauntiness Vera Lynn's never had.

"Well you couldn't expect him to leave her on her own," Mum had said reasonably. "And you didn't want her here."

"I should think not! It's difficult enough feeding five of us, without another two." This was before Auntie Thelma's parcel had arrived.

So Sam came for tea the first Sunday in the New Year, and immediately upset Gan by refusing a glass of her wine. "I've signed the pledge," he told her rather pompously, and she was so annoyed that she poured Mum and herself another large glass which Mum didn't dare refuse.

Sam had an indignant tale to tell. "One of Mum's chickens was stolen just before Christmas. So she called a policeman and he followed a trail of chicken feathers which led to this fellow's hut. Inside, he found a pile of ashes and bones and the man had the cheek to tell him they were the remains of a rabbit."

Gan said flippantly, "He should have said it was the one-legged goose."

Sam was utterly bewildered. "One-legged . . . what do you mean, Mrs Cooper?"

"It was a recipe in one of the women's magazines. Goose with one leg. You're supposed to make it with a small leg of lamb, but I reckon a big rabbit's leg would do."

None of us really saw the joke, which Gan thought very funny. Mum hastily asked Sam, "What happened, was he taken to court?"

"He was, but in my opinion he was let off too lightly," Sam replied stiffly. "He was bound over and had to pay fifteen shillings costs. And it's left poor Mother very nervous, though she tries hard not to let me see it."

More and more, Gan began showing her dislike of Sam. Usually, Mum was quick to defend him. But when he, in turn, criticised her friend Debbie, they fell out.

Mum had taken him to tea at Debbie's house. Unfortunately, Debbie had been in one of her more outrageous moods, telling a tale over the tea-table which had shocked Sam into a disapproving silence.

"It was really embarrassing," Mum admitted over a cup of tea with Gan. "The more he sulked, the more she spun her yarns. Then on the way to the ferry he had the nerve to tell me he didn't want me to see her again . . . that she was no better than she should be. I told him, she's on the next machine to me in the Dockyard, and I see her every day. Anyway, I like her."

Gan was full of sympathy. "Fancy saying that about a friend of yours," she indignantly exclaimed, forgetting she had once said exactly the same about Debbie. "I wouldn't let him get away with that, Ida."

"I didn't. I told him, Debbie stays my friend. So he didn't ask me out for next week."

Gan slowly finished her tea, before saying gruffly, "Never mind, there are plenty more fish in the sea. Come on, let's hear this tale Debbie was spinning."

Mum put down her cup and chuckled. Neither Diane, Jill nor I looked up from our game of Old Maid, as we sat on the rag rug in front of the fire.

"Well, it seems she and Dora Shingle went to one of these Forces Recreation Centres, where they provide

"He said he'd give half a dozen pairs of nylons
for a dish of real English dumplings."

meals for men from overseas. They got talking to an American, who said he'd give half a dozen pairs of nylons for a dish of English dumplings."

Laughter choked in Gan's throat. "A dish of . . . you're not telling me they really thought . . ."

"Oh no, of course they thought he must mean . . . you know . . . but not . . . not . . ." Mum hesitated. "They weren't sure whether he meant a . . . it-b of anky-h anky-p or the whole aboodle-c."

"Snap," Jill suddenly shouted. "It's Old Maid we're supposed to be playing," Diane said, exasperated. "Betty, I'm waiting to take from you." My interest in the game had momentarily flagged. I knew what "hanky-panky" meant.

"Of course," Mum was saying. "Debbie said she couldn't . . . whatever it was he wanted. She had her husband to think of, but Dora's hubby left her years ago. So they agreed Dora would invite him to her flat, and any nylons she got she would share with Debbie, in exchange for half a box of American cigarettes Debbie had won in a raffle the week before."

"Well, you'll never believe this! It turned out he wasn't after . . . you know what! He wanted just what he had said, a plateful of suet dumplings in gravy just like he'd heard English people had every Sunday. Debbie said she nearly wet herself laughing at Dora's face when she told her."

Gan chortled. "So didn't she get the nylons?"

"Yes, she did, and he's coming round next Sunday for his dumplings."

I was staring at Mum in fascination, half shocked at the first of Debbie's risqué stories I had understood. Turning my head, I caught Gan's eye, and knew that she knew I knew.

"You sly little madam," she said softly. "I might have known it wouldn't be long before *you* cottoned on to your Mum's and my private conversations. Well, don't you dare repeat anything you hear in this house, is that clear?"

I assured her it was. In any case, I didn't know anyone to repeat to, apart from Diane, which I did at the first chance I had.

Air-raids had eased off after the terrible Spring blitz of 1941. Not long after Christmas, we had our first raid for months, long enough for us to have got out of the way of them. We were completely unprepared.

Urgently prodded awake by Gan . . . the siren hadn't woken me . . . I leapt out of bed, trying to find my shoes in the dark until Gan, who was propelling a comatose Diane in front of her, yelled at me to "Forget them and come quickly, can't you hear the planes coming?"

With Mum herding Jill, we snatched our coats from the peg on the back of the kitchen door and hurried down the garden to the Anderson shelter.

Mum and Gan hadn't been able to find the torch though we didn't need one outside. It was a bright moonlit night. But we had to feel our way into the dark, musty-smelling hole in the ground, an arch of corrugated iron camouflaged from the air by the grass which grew over it. A piece of old lino covered the earth floor, but there was an inch of water over it, striking a chill through my bare feet. We huddled onto bare wire-mesh beds on either side of the door. Gan would normally have brought the kitchen rag rugs to cover them, but she had uncharacteristically panicked.

It was so miserable in there, the raid almost took second place in our minds. When the All Clear finally sounded we crept thankfully back to the house, to a cup of Oxo each and a scolding, "That'll teach you to throw your shoes about all over the place, Betty," from Gan. But she gave me her woolly scarf to wrap my frozen feet in.

Jill developed a bad, chesty cough which lingered for the rest of the winter, from being taken out of her warm bed into the cold that night. Gan declared, "That's the last time we go in that godforsaken hole, Ida. If the raids are coming back, we'll stay where we are."

"Do you mean in the bedroom?"

"Yes. Raids are a darn sight less frightening if you can see what's going on," Gan said firmly. "Shut in that hole, with the din bouncing off that corrugated iron, is enough to give anybody the wind up . . . not to mention pneumonia." So when the next raid woke us from our sleep, we sat on Mum and Gan's bed in the dark, watching the display of searchlights criss-crossing the sky from the window, and listening to the accompanying noisy chorus of planes, guns and bombs.

If Gan's theory worked, it did so only for her. We children were petrified, huddled on the bed in silent fear, but knowing we must hide it from Sir Percy.

Raids might be less frequent and shorter than the ones we remembered from 1941. But to us, what they lacked of their former, relentless ferocity, they now made up for in sheer din. It was a great deal noisier living opposite Devonport Dockyard than it had been in the relatively sheltered creek of Millbrook.

With the return of air-raids, after such a long respite, Gan seemed to get back her spirit of camaraderie with her upstairs neighbour.

Mr Shipley worked in London, where his wife and son occasionally visited him. Through seeing less of her neighbour, Gan began to appreciate her more. She often invited the Shipleys down for a cup of tea and, to Diane's and my joy, allowed us to accept Mrs Shipley's invitation to go to the Lawn with her and Peter.

The Lawn had once been part of a large house at the water's edge, not far from our home. It was now a public park, with a tidal pool separating it from the River Tamar, and with tall trees at its perimeter.

To Diane and me, it was heaven to be free of Gan's censorious eye, to feel the free rein of Mrs Shipley's easy chaperonage. Too easy, I'm afraid. On the first day she took us, out of her sight amongst the trees, all three of us were interfered with by a benign-looking gentleman whose walking stick and grey hair had encouraged us to see him as a grandfather figure.

Diane, Peter and I had climbed a tree. Standing below us, his kindly eyes twinkling up at us, the man insisted on lifting us down.

Hurrying back across the Lawn to find Mrs Shipley, I blurted out to a subdued Diane, "That man . . . he put his hand where he shouldn't." I think she was relieved it hadn't been just her. "Oh Betty," she whispered, "he did it to me too."

I looked at Peter, half my size, his short, chubby legs working twice as fast as ours to keep up with us. I said, "That man, Peter, did he touch your . . . ?" I stopped. Whatever did boys call theirs?

"Yes, he did." Peter was panting. "My Mum won't half be cross. She's always telling me not to."

Cross? We knew his Mother would be horror-stricken. And she was.

"Oh Good Lord," she wailed. "Whatever will Mrs Cooper say? She'll blame me. She'll never let you come out with me again."

Diane and I exchanged glances of dismay. We spoke in unison. "We won't tell her," we promised. And we never did.

CHAPTER
TEN

"Is your Journey Really Necessary?"

(Government poster)

I was always conscious of how my family seemed to lack other relations. Children I knew had aunts and uncles, often just down the street, and cousins with whom they played. Our contact with relations was solely through the post.

We had the most regular correspondence with Mum's friend Auntie Thelma, in America. Though she was no real relation she was very good to us, continuing to send us food and clothing parcels throughout the rest of the war. We never forgot that first tin of Spam, which we loved, and the jar of peanut butter, which we didn't. But it wasn't wasted. Mum made it into delicious peanut brownies, that is, as long as she got it before Gan commandeered it for one of her substitute recipes. Gan had an implacable conviction that for every recipe ingredient, there must be an alternative. So we had treacle pudding, malt loaf, and chocolate dough cake, all with peanut butter substituting for the treacle, malt and cocoa.

We always opened Auntie Thelma's parcels in excited anticipation, but still I wished for an aunt to visit like

Cynthia, who sat next to me at school, or an uncle home from the Front, like Vera Todd.

It was therefore with immense excitement that we went to visit our Nottingham relatives that summer, for the first time.

Gan had two brothers and two sisters who had never moved from the area in and around Nottingham, and who still had their extended families living nearby. Auntie Lizzie had invited us to visit them the previous year, at the height of the Plymouth blitz. Now, we were in a financial position to accept her invitation.

But Auntie Lizzie and Gan had since had a row, none the less rancorous for having been conducted by letter. Luckily for us, the usual practice prevailed. When Gan fell out with one sister, she invariably became on bosom terms with the other. So we went to stay with Auntie Ida and Uncle Charlie in Nottingham.

We set out to catch a late afternoon train from Plymouth, on a bright sunny day, perfectly in tune with our spirits. We arrived at North Road station to find it thronging with servicemen and women. Mum and Gan struggled through noisy groups of them with our luggage. Diane and I, each tightly holding one of Jill's hands, anxiously tried to keep the top of Mum's head in sight as the rest of her was blotted out by ever-moving Navy and Air Force blue uniforms. We finally reached the platform we wanted, and sat on our luggage beneath a large poster asking if our journey was really necessary, to wait for the Bristol train.

It arrived very late and very full. At the sight of corridors already crammed with people who could not

We sat beneath a large poster,
to wait for the Bristol train.

get a seat, I began to panic again, and clutched desperately to Gan's sleeve until she shook me off with an irritated, "For Heaven's sake, hang on to Jill and do something useful."

To my immense relief we all managed to squeeze onto the train. My nose was pressed against the window of a compartment. It was full of sailors. Five were crammed along each seat, two occupied the overhead luggage racks and several more squatted on the floor, squashed between knees and kitbags.

In the packed corridor there was no room for Mum and Gan to sit on our luggage, but we children were able to. As the train began to roll out of Plymouth a sailor came out of the compartment and said to Gan,

I waved through the window at Jill,
and wondered why Gan was looking so grim.

"You're welcome to my seat, Missus. I'm happy enough to stand." His cheerful grin slewed from Gan to Mum.

So Gan thankfully squeezed herself between two sailors, Jill on her knee, while Mum stood tightly squashed between the compartment window and the kindly sailor, who gallantly put his arm around her every time the train lurched. I waved through the window at Jill, and wondered why Gan was looking so grim.

By the time we all stumbled off the train at Bristol, each of us had suffered a mood change from the one we had started out with. Jill was weepy, from having had to sit so still for so long, on Gan's unsympathetic knee. Diane and I were cramped after what had seemed an interminable crouch on the suitcase, and Mum and Gan appeared to have fallen out. They started as soon as they were within earshot of each other.

"Well, I've never been so ashamed in all my life," Gan hissed. She snatched up the big suitcase which Diane and I had carried off the train with much effort and promptly abandoned us, barking over her shoulder as she stalked after Mum and Jill, "Keep up with us."

Jill, who had made a quick dash for Mum as soon as she was out of Gan's reach, to grab frantically at the only thing she could reach which was Mum's shoulder bag, now found her other hand snatched up by Gan.

"Whatever were you thinking of, letting that sailor maul you?"

Mum's usually gentle voice sharpened. "What do you mean, maul me?" Jill, hurried off her short legs by the two irate women, cast an alarmed glance back at us.

We could just see the whites of her eyes as we hurried towards the platform for the Nottingham train.

"Just what I say, you silly little madam!" Gan was getting out of breath but wouldn't let go of Jill's hand.

Old habits die hard. Apparently forgetting that their secret code had been cracked, she bit at Mum, "We could all ee-s you through the indow-w. We all saw . . . where that ighter's-bl ands-h were."

"What do you mean, where they were?" Mum's voice was indignant. "We hadn't an inch to spare in the corridor. He had no room to put them anywhere."

"Oh no?" Gan snapped back sarcastically. "So that's why he had to ut-p them on your um . . . erriere-d? He didn't know what else to do with them? I've never heard such a cock-and-bull tale in my life. I tell you, my girl, I didn't know where to look."

Mum took a sharp breath and withdrew into dignified silence. Diane and I exchanged scandalised looks, and Jill burst into tears.

"There, now look what you've done." Mum stopped so suddenly, to bend down and comfort our little sister, Diane and I cannoned into them. It gave Gan an excuse to redirect her anger.

"Watch where you're going," she snapped at me. "How many times have I told you, not to walk right on our heels." We reached the platform we wanted and then spent some of the most miserable hours I can remember. It gradually got darker and colder, as we sat once more on the hard suitcases. The station was blacked out, with nothing but a dim blue light here and there. Nothing was open, nowhere to buy a drink, no

110

waiting room to sit in, and there was a long queue outside the only toilet. The train we were waiting for had been cancelled and the time we waited for the next one seemed never-ending. I was so tired by the time it arrived I have only a dim memory of being pushed onto it and being offered, with my sisters, an airman's knee to sit on. I fell asleep, half-way through my airman's thickly accented account of his daughter like me, back in Czechoslovakia, and despite the terrible smell of his breath, until the train pulled in at Nottingham at four o'clock in the morning, when we had expected to arrive at eleven.

We went in a taxi to Auntie Ida's house. Too weary to feel any excitement at meeting this eagerly wanted aunt, who had anxiously waited up all night for us, we all went straight to bed.

Poor Auntie Ida. All three of us children were sick, all over the clean sheets. And as if that were not bad enough, I had a nightmare. I crawled, shaking, out of bed and onto the unfamiliar landing to look for Mum, forgot we were not in our downstairs flat at home and fell down the stairs with a crash that once again wakened the whole household. Luckily for me, there was a bend in the stairs, so I only went half-way down.

It was an inauspicious start, but worse was to come. During the first week of our visit, catastrophe after catastrophe struck, most of them my fault. It was as though an evil jinx had attached itself to me, and I could not shake it off. I couldn't believe what was happening to me and I suspect Mum and Gan were

111

equally flabbergasted. If I'd been a dedicated juvenile delinquent I couldn't have caused more damage.

The first one involved the wash-basin in the bathroom. Used to putting up a foot at a time to wash in the old stone sink at home, I did the same in Auntie Ida's wall-mounted bowl, and brought it crashing to the floor. Then, at dinner, we had plums and custard for dessert and I didn't know what to do with the stones, so I swallowed the lot. When Auntie Ida looked at my plate, she was horrified. Her endorsement of Gan's grim promise of a dose of medicine, was, I knew, from real concern. Looking at Gan's angry face, it was clear she saw it as a punishment I richly deserved and my heart sank. She never shouted at us in front of our Aunt and Uncle, but we knew we would pay for any misdemeanours when we went to bed. That night, she brought out the dreaded "Ippycak" and gave me a double dose, which made me sick without having any immediate effect on the seven plum-stones I had swallowed.

Gan must have got over her annoyance with me, because she took me with her to visit her brother Claude's wife, Auntie Annie, while Mum and my sisters went to see one of Mum's cousins.

Auntie Annie shared Gan's interest in the spirit world. The two women huddled together over a crystal ball set on a piece of dark-green velvet, and sent me to amuse myself in the front room.

A huge glass cabinet stood on a narrow shelf, full of curios. It overhung the shelf, but I didn't realise the danger. I pulled it open and the cupboard began to topple over. I just managed to spring back out of the way before it crashed down at my feet.

I had time for no more than an agonised plea for divine help before Auntie Annie and Gan came rushing in. To my astonished relief, they believed my story that as I looked at the cupboard from the door, it had fallen.

Gan's voice was low and dramatic. "Someone was looking after her, Annie," she said solemnly. "She was an Instrument. It was meant to be."

Auntie Annie was remarkably philosophical. "Well, I reckon it must have been my old Mum gave it a shove, Mab," she said cheerfully. "She knew I never could abide Claude's mother's knick-knacks."

I was still shaking. She drew me among the debris and said kindly. "See if there's something not broken you'd like to have, Betty," and I was so grateful to God, I chose a little model of the Nativity.

After that, I walked everywhere as though on eggshells, and my disasters came to an end. Jill caused one, by fiddling with the Yale lock on the front door, so that we couldn't get back in, and Uncle Charlie had to break a window. Diane was the only non-offender, which was probably because Gan told her menacingly, after the door episode, "And don't you dare think it's your turn next, because I'll flatten you if you do."

Our second week was lovely. I found it both delightful and confusing to find we had so many relatives. Auntie Ida was a plump, comfortable woman, as sweet-tempered as Mum, her namesake. Uncle Charlie was rather austere. That may have been because of the wash-basin and the window but from our limited knowledge of men . . . Mum's friend Sam was the only other man we knew . . . we just thought it was normal male behaviour.

We were taken to meet numerous cousins, uncles and aunts, and despite Gan's insisting she did not want to visit Auntie Lizzie, Auntie Ida was equally insistent that we went.

Auntie Lizzie was a quick, small woman, with long black hair plaited around her head. Uncle Harry was big, bushy-eyebrowed, very kind to three tongue-tied little girls who were only too conscious of Gan's stiff behaviour as she entered the house. But we need not have worried. Auntie Ida drew her two older sisters together and in no time Gan was talking her usual nineteen to the dozen.

Uncle Harry took Mum and us children into the garden. Through the open window, we could hear Gan holding forth. "Yes, she still has her gentleman-friend," she was telling her sisters. "He's a very nice type of man and thinks the world of Ida."

We heard Auntie Ida's placid voice. "I thought it was all over between them."

"No, no. It was all a misunderstanding. He's as keen as ever and in fact, he wanted her to stay with him and his mother, a very superior lady, while the rest of us came to visit you, but of course Ida wouldn't have missed this trip for anything. But it goes to show how smitten he is, he can hardly bear to let her out of his sight."

"And how do you get on with him, Mab?" asked Auntie Lizzie.

114

"Like a house on fire," Gan answered promptly. "Sam is always eager for an invite to tea. I don't think he gets cooking like mine at home."

My head swivelled to look at Mum. Overriding my surprise to hear that she and Sam had made up their quarrel, was astonishment that Gan now quite liked him.

Mum's face was very pink. She said loudly to Uncle Harry, who was slightly deaf, "Shall we walk to the bottom of the garden, Uncle? The kids aren't used to a garden like this. All we have in ours is an Anderson shelter."

CHAPTER
ELEVEN

"Potatoes give more energy than meat."

(Ministry of Food)

The journey home from Nottingham was as miserable as it had been getting there. It was another overnight journey, with long delays in cold, dark stations, though outside a bright moon shone over Bristol. We had just squeezed onto the crowded Plymouth train when the sirens wailed and passengers were invited to take cover if they wished, as the train would not move until the All Clear. Nobody moved, all unwilling to risk losing their place on the train.

We eventually arrived at North Road station in Plymouth in the early hours, all of us worn out. Buses had not yet resumed services, after their 9.30p.m. curfew, and we got a taxi to Torpoint ferry, where we had an hour's wait.

Our final crawl home, through the darkened little town was utterly depressing, with not a word spoken among us until we reached home.

We children still had some school holiday left, much to Gan's disgust. Mum was back at work on the Monday. She came home with news from Debbie of a bad raid on Plymouth while we had been away.

The first alert had been at 9 o'clock in the evening, but turned out to be a false alarm over two Spitfires. People went to bed and were woken by another alert after midnight. The All Clear went shortly afterwards when people went back to bed.

"It was one of the dirtiest tricks the Jerries have ever played," Debbie had indignantly exclaimed. "Do you know what they did? They waited for some of our bombers, coming back from a raid on them, then sneaked in behind them, with no searchlights and the balloons lowered to let our boys in. They'd dropped their flares and bombs before the sirens had time to warn people, and many of them didn't get to the shelters in time."

Debbie was particularly upset because one of her friends was killed, a part-time fire-woman, as well as the wife of one of her Dad's Home Guard colleagues. But we all shared her indignation. It never occurred to any of us at the time, that our airmen were probably playing the same dirty tricks on the Germans.

We were glad to get back to school when the time came. We knew Gan hated having us at home under her feet. As I had dreaded, my first cooking lesson in the new term brought on a renewal of the one-sided feud between Gan and Mrs Proctor.

It began when Mrs Proctor gave us a recipe for Partisan Pie. We had to write out a list of ingredients, which was sub-divided into one each for body-building foods, energy foods, and protective foods. She said we were to use our imaginations, but must choose foods from each list to make a pie.

The trouble lay in their different interpretations of food values. Gan claimed she recognised Mrs Proctor's list of ingredients as one of the Ministry of Food's regularly published newspaper articles. Normally, she hadn't a good word to say for Lord Woolton. It was a different matter when there was an apparent discrepancy between Mrs Proctor's list and his.

Her eye ran down my list. "Well, for a start she's got milk in the wrong list," she said. "Milk is the best of the body-building foods. You can have a quarter pint." She crossed it off one list and added it to another.

"And potatoes should be in the energy foods." Another cross.

I began to get anxious. "I'll need flour for a pie," I pleaded and with a loud, resigned sigh she ticked off flour from my energy list, and scanned the one for protective foods. "Green vegetables are the best," she decided. "You can have a slice of cabbage."

I peered at my list over her shoulder and ventured, "What about marge?"

"I haven't any to spare," Gan said shortly. "You'll have to make the pastry with milk." I knew the futility of arguing with her, despite an uneasy conviction that Mrs Proctor would consider my ingredients inadequate.

My next cookery lesson confirmed my fears. Mrs Proctor moved round the tables, inspecting the ingredients laid out in front of each girl. She made a prolonged stop in front of mine, then asked, "Is it to be potato pastry, Betty?"

118

"No, the potato is the energy to go in the pie," I explained. I had thought it through on the way to school. "It's going to be a batter pie."

Mrs Proctor considered. "In that case, you need eggs," she said, then took pity at my crestfallen face. "It's all right Betty, I'll give you a spoonful of dried egg," she said kindly.

My pie was so successful, nicely risen and brown, Mrs Proctor used it as a good example of cooking in wartime. Exhilarated that my potential disaster had turned into a triumph, I proudly handed it over to Gan when I got home and repeated Mrs Proctor's remarks.

Gan exploded straight after I got to the bit about making something of very little, and before I could mention that my pie was judged the most appetising looking.

"What does she mean, 'very little'?" she demanded. "They were the ingredients she asked for, weren't they?"

"Yes, but — she meant without any fat or meat, like most of the other girls brought." Too late, I wished I'd kept Mrs Proctor's praise to myself. As always, the slightest suspicion that she was being patronised infuriated Gan.

She snapped, "If she's got nothing better to do than belittle what I send, I've done with her," and all my self-satisfaction evaporated. With a heavy heart, I thought of the next week's cookery list in my pocket, which included at least two ingredients I knew she wouldn't have.

But I didn't know the worst until the following week. Not only did I have to take a chopped apple instead of sultanas and a teaspoon of cocoa as a substitute for mixed spice. When I asked for our cheese ration, which Gan allowed Mrs Proctor to buy, she sharply told me, "She's not having any more," and bundled me out of the door.

I was very upset. All the way to school I desperately tried to think of a way out of this one, and inevitably the only solution which occurred to me was more lies.

"Gan's not very well again," I gabbled, before Mrs Proctor could ask me about the cheese. "I'm sorry, Mrs Proctor, but she's got so thin and weak, the Doctor says she must eat all our cheese ration herself, even though she hates it. She's really sorry."

For the first time, I wasn't absolutely sure Mrs Proctor believed me.

Gan had a serious fall-out with Mrs Crisp. It was so bad even her more genteel neighbour raised her voice, and since Gan had left the kitchen door ajar, we heard the whole of this row at first hand.

Gan had gone to hang out some washing, and by the greatest misfortune she happened to look over the fence into the Crisps' back garden. Even worse, Mrs Crisp came out while she was looking.

"Well!" It needed no more than that one, loudly exclaimed word, for us to know there was going to be trouble. Mum exchanged a startled glance with Diane and me, her cup of tea spilling half way to her lips. Six-year-old Jill clutched her shabby Teddy tightly to her chest, anxious eyes betraying that old, familiar apprehension we all shared as we stared at Gan's stiff back through the kitchen window.

"So that's what you do with it!"

Mrs Crisp's face, just visible over the garden fence, registered bewilderment at her neighbour's angry tone, before we saw her eyes slew down to where Gan's accusing finger pointed. She looked up, her colour heightened, but without losing any of her habitual air of lady-like superiority.

"What are you talking about, Mrs Cooper?" she asked pleasantly.

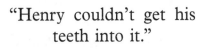

"Henry couldn't get his teeth into it."

"You know damn well what I'm talking about. So that's what you do with the cake I give you."

Mrs Crisp tried to be conciliatory. "I'm really sorry, Mrs Cooper, but I'm afraid it had gone stale and rather than waste it, we let Pip have it."

"Stale?" Gan retorted angrily. "I only gave it you yesterday. It hadn't had time to go stale."

"I'm afraid it had." Mrs Crisp's voice was polite but firm. "Henry couldn't get his teeth into it. I'm sorry, Mrs Cooper, but at least we didn't waste it."

"Didn't waste it? When I think of all those poor starving souls in Italy — they'd have given anything for it."

"Not for this they wouldn't." Mrs Crisp suddenly swooped down and picked up the piece of cake. "I'm sure they'd rather eat the cats." She was referring to a recent newspaper article claiming that all the cats in Rome had been eaten.

The silence was so acute in our kitchen, we could all hear the choking sound Gan made. The atmosphere was hardly less electric than that between the two women. I remembered when we lived in Millbrook, more than once having a race with Diane to see who could get to the outside lavatory first, to escape one of Gan's outbursts. There was no such escape here. We'd have had to push past her to reach it.

Gan's tone was as stiff as her back. "I'll have you know, Mrs Crisp, you could be prosecuted. It's against the law to feed dogs with human food."

By this time, Mrs Crisp was as angry as Gan. "Human food, yes, Mrs Cooper. But that cake wasn't fit for human consumption."

"I'll have you know, a woman was fined £1 in Devonport last week for feeding cake to dogs. You can be thankful I'm not a vindictive woman, or else I'd report you."

Mrs Crisp snapped, her tone now as shrill as Gan's was bellicose. "Then I suggest you go ahead and report me. And it wasn't cake, it was bread she fed to the dogs."

"Then it's even worse, what you've done. When I think of all those good, healthy ingredients I put into it."

"Oh, for Heaven's sake! Even my Pip wouldn't eat it. I shall put it where I should have put it in the first place — in the pig-bin." And with that Mrs Crisp stalked back into her house, leaving Gan without even the satisfaction of the last word.

Gan's face was scarlet when she came in. "Did you hear all that?" she demanded, rather unnecessarily. "Well, that's it. That's the last time I deprive our kids to give good cake to that woman." And she kept her word.

"Even my Pip wouldn't eat it!"

CHAPTER
TWELVE

"My British Buddy, we're as different as can be.
You think you're winning the war
and I think it's me."

(Wartime song)

We began to see more and more American soldiers, and after feeling for so long that we stood alone, they were very welcome. People cheered them wildly when they marched in the Wings for Victory parade in Plymouth. But still they seemed a race apart, often viewed with suspicion by the more insular Cornish.

There were a number of newspaper articles expressing concern at the effect these glamorous strangers were having on the morals of some young women. "We shall never win the war if we allow this behaviour," warned one Cornish parish council.

There was even concern expressed by the Home Secretary, in Parliament's continuing pressure on the Cornish police to recruit more women police officers ... "in view of the lax conduct on the part of young women." The Cornish police resisted, as they had for the previous three or four years, but by the following year they had bowed to pressure and had agreed to recruit twenty young women.

The G.I.s were generous, often keeping their girl-friends supplied with very welcome nylons. But some girls took advantage of their generosity. Debbie's friend Dora was caught after getting fifty pairs of nylons from an American soldier, then selling them.

"She was fined twice over — once for acquiring and once for supplying," Mum told Gan. "And Debbie was furious because all Dora's customers were fined too. Debbie had to pay £1."

"Serve Dora right," Gan said promptly. "She shouldn't be so greedy. What about the American . . . was he fined?"

"I think he was dealt with by his own officers," Mum said. "But in any case, Debbie says she doesn't think he actually got any money for them."

Gan said grimly, "I bet he didn't. And I bet they cost Dora more than a dish of suety dumplings this time."

A serious incident occurred in a small Cornish town which caused a dent in Anglo-American relations, before it was severely dealt with by the American military authorities. Twenty G.I.s broke out of their camp with guns, and came to the normally quiet town on a Sunday morning, to begin a shooting battle with their own military police. They were all arrested without any Cornish people being hurt, but they had injured two of their own military police. They were eventually court-martialled and sent back to the States.

More often, people simply found it difficult to understand the free and easy manners of the G.I.s. One Saturday we caught the ferry to Devonport and it had just pulled away when a group of American soldiers

They pelted down the steep ferry slope so fast, one of them was up to his thighs in the Tamar before he could stop.

came racing to catch it. They pelted down the steep ferry slipway so fast, one of them was up to his thighs in the Tamar before he could stop.

"Hi — come back," they shouted. "Wait for us," while we stood on the prow with other passengers and watched them in an embarrassed silence, wondering at their complete lack of inhibition.

On another occasion, the Americans scored. We were waiting in a long queue for the ferry when a DUKW (an amphibious motor vehicle), swept past us, took to the water and crossed to Devonport ahead of us, its crew unable to conceal an understandable feeling of smugness.

On the whole though, the Americans were seen as a kindly, if rather eccentric race, good to have as allies.

Mum didn't seem to come home with any risqué tales from Debbie any more. Either she now kept them until Diane and I had gone to bed, or Debbie had run out of them. She did tell Gan one day that Debbie knew a rude version of "Bless 'Em All", but didn't tell it in front of us. I thought at first I had guessed the key word. It was the only really bad word I knew. I had once seen it scribbled all over a wall, dozens of times, as though the writer himself had just come across it. Mum didn't know what it meant when I asked, but Gan was horrified.

"Don't you ever dare repeat that word again," she said sharply. "It's the most disgusting word in the English language."

So of course I never forgot it, though I found out, much later, that there was another one I didn't know, which was the one used in "Bless 'Em All".

Mum often had stories about the people she worked with. One of the women on a machine near her got into serious trouble over a letter she had received from her husband, who was in the Navy. He had used a form of code to let her know when his ship should be arriving in Plymouth.

"He put dots under certain letters," Mum explained. "And they've been fined £20. Poor Meg, she'll be working a while before she pays that off. And goodness knows what trouble her husband will get into."

Mum's tale reminded Gan of a newspaper story she had recently read, headed "American troops suffer from 'Code in the Head'". Their letters home, too, were censored. The account told of one soldier in North Africa who had sent five letters to his mother, trying to tell her that he was in Tunis. But she did not receive his letters in the correct sequence. Her efforts to spell out his code resulted in "Nutsi", which she could not find on the map of Africa.

She could not find Nutsi on the map of Africa.

"It's to be hoped he had more wits than his mother," was Gan's scathing comment.

Mum recounted another Dockyard incident with a great deal less sympathy. "One of Jack Dolon's ex-mates has just been sent to prison for two months," she told Gan. Jack Dolon was an overseer at the Dockyard.

Gan was startled. "What on earth has he done?"

The man had committed the serious offence of missing his fire-watch duty. "He was supposed to report to the Dockyard every eight days," said Mum. "But one duty he turned up drunk and was stopped at the gate. Jack says Les has got hard labour and it serves him right. The whole Dockyard could burn down if there were more like him."

Fire-watching was considered very important, often the means by which fires were prevented from spreading out of control. None of us gave any thought to poor old Les, perhaps ending up on Dartmoor, breaking stones, just for getting drunk.

One evening we were invited up to the Shipleys' flat for supper. Invitations out were very rare except for Mum, of course, who was still going out with Sam most weekends. Gan would not admit to any expected pleasure but we children were very excited and talked of nothing else, until Gan had had enough.

"For Heaven's sake — if you kids don't shut up we'll leave you in bed when we go upstairs," she threatened. "Anyone would think you'd never been anywhere before." Since we always took Gan's threats seriously, Diane and I instantly shut up.

But nothing could diminish the thrilled anticipation with which we followed Mum and Gan upstairs and into the Shipleys' brightly decorated flat.

Mrs Shipley was very fond of yellow. It was everywhere — the thick curtains over the window and the shiny cushions on a large settee, with the door painted to match. On the wall hung a picture of a vase of sunflowers. It was vastly different to our colour scheme downstairs, where Gan favoured brown as a colour that "didn't show the dirt".

Mrs Shipley was a nicely relaxed hostess. She set Diane and me to play cards with Peter, while Jill was given a brick jigsaw, to her huge delight. And she and Gan got on like a house on fire, with Mum content to be a listener. Mrs Shipley asked Mum kindly questions about Sam and Gan answered them. In between two games of Snap, which I lost, and a game of Strip Jack Naked, which I left to Diane to explain to Peter, I picked up several interesting snippets about Sam and his mother.

"He looks very nice." Mrs Shipley smiled at Mum and Gan said heartily, "He *is* nice, and he thinks the world of Ida. I think he'd live at our place if he could. He's always glad of a bit of home cooking, isn't he Ida?"

"Yes," Mum agreed. "Of course, his mother . . ." "She is a very superior lady," Gan finished for her. "But of course, that doesn't always mean homely. He couldn't get enough of my Mock Goose last time he came to tea."

"Is that one of Lord Woolton's recipes?" "No, I don't always bother with him," Gan said loftily. "I have an old recipe book, you can borrow it if you like. You need sage and onion stuffing, haricot beans and cold mashed potato. I think Sam likes it better than the real thing, doesn't he?" She looked at Mum who said hastily, "Well, I don't think they get too many geese on his farm. They have chickens, but it's mostly a milking farm."

130

Gan told Mrs Shipley, "They lost quite a few of their cattle a few months ago. Do you remember that bad raid, when the woman down the road was hurt by hot shrapnel? Well, some incendiaries landed in the byre, setting fire to the hay, and half a dozen cows were burned to death, poor things. Sam's mother was very upset."

"I'm sure she would be." I heard a hint of mischief softening Mrs Shipley's voice and my head shot up. "Do you get on with her, Ida?"

I looked at Mum. She was looking at Gan, hesitatingly, and Gan promptly helped her out. "She's very fond of Ida, but you know how it is with an only son." The slow shake of her head said only too plainly that *she* knew, even if Mum didn't.

"Well, you'll have to get her sorted out before you get married," said Mrs Shipley cheerfully, to which Gan firmly answered, "It's early days for all that. They've got a lot of thinking to do . . . it would be a big change for all of us, and we have the girls to think of." Thought of the girls prompted her to shoot a hard glance at me but, long practised, I was absorbed in the card game before she had moved her head.

When it was time to leave, Gan graciously accepted a recipe from Mrs Shipley for Portman Pudding, which our neighbour said was delicious and hardly used any sugar, and Gan promised to send up her old recipe book, which had belonged to her grandmother.

We had all enjoyed ourselves, even Gan, who had nothing more disparaging to say, after she had inspected the Portman Pudding recipe than, "I tell you what, Ida, that Lord Woolton is a fraud. This pudding recipe has exactly the same ingredients as Carrot Cookies. He must think we're all dense."

Gan was still at odds with our next-door neighbour. An event happened involving both her and Mrs Crisp, which might have been expected to draw them together. In fact, it had the opposite effect.

Gan was waiting outside the back door one Monday afternoon, as Diane and I came home from school. We could see from right down the road that she was agitated.

"Did you see anyone as you came out of school?" she called as soon as we were within earshot.

Diane and I stared at one another, slow on the uptake as usual.

Gan gave an exasperated sigh. "For Heaven's sake! Did you see anyone suspicious — someone carrying a bundle of washing?"

We hadn't and she poured out an indignant tale as we followed her into the house. Apparently, she had gone to meet Jill from school and when they got back, her washing had disappeared from the line.

"Would you believe it," she fumed. "I was only gone ten minutes. And it would've only been five if you'd come straight out of school," she snapped at poor Jill, who was trying to melt into the background.

Gan glanced out of the kitchen window. "Go and bring those pegs in, before they come back for them," she ordered me, and I hurried out to do her bidding.

132

As I was collecting them from the line, Mrs Crisp looked over the fence. "Betty," she called, "has your Gran lost her washing too?"

I stopped and stared. "Yes, she has, Mrs Crisp."

Our neighbour had suffered the same misfortune. "And Mrs Elliot across the back and goodness knows how many more."

I stopped to listen to Mrs Crisp's tale of woe and told her a few details of Gan's, before I became aware of Gan glaring at me through the kitchen window.

"I'll have to go now," I hastily told our neighbour. "Gan is waiting for these pegs."

"What did she want?" Gan demanded before I'd even closed the door.

"She's lost her washing too. And Mrs Elliot."

The news seemed to mollify Gan. "Well," she exclaimed, "so somebody's been clearing out the whole road. Has she lost much?"

I knew she meant Mrs Crisp and eager to mollify her a bit more I said, "Yes, she's lost a hand-embroidered bedspread, all done in pastel colours, and an Irish linen tablecloth, as well as lots of other things. But I told her we'd only lost a pair of patched sheets and some pillowcases that were scorched anyway. Oh, and Jill's pyjamas that were so worn, you said they were only fit to be used for dusters."

Gan wasn't looking as pleased as I'd expected. I quickly added, "Mrs Crisp said she was glad you hadn't lost anything really valuable."

There was an absolute silence as Gan stared at me. The high colour in her cheeks had started spreading alarmingly all down her neck and I recognised the signs. Without understanding why, I knew she was more angry with me than the washing-line thief.

Mum found herself involved as soon as she came home that evening. She had taken off her coat and said ruefully, "Look at that!" indicating a jagged tear in her trouser leg, "I caught it on a nail sticking out of some wooden boxes, as we walked through the Yard."

Gan was sarcastic. "Let me have them and I'll hang them out on the line," she retorted. "That'll be something else of ours only fit for dusters."

Mum was taken aback. She shot a questioning look at my sisters and me, wondering which one of us had upset Gan. We were all subdued, but by Gan's smouldering glances in my direction, I expect she guessed it was me.

CHAPTER
THIRTEEN

"They Can't Blackout the Moon" — Wartime song

*(On a bright, moonlit night,
people talked of a "Bombers' Moon")*

One November night we were wakened abruptly by the
siren, the drone of planes overhead and the noisy explosion
of bombs intermingled with heavy gunfire, all happening
at once. There was no time to come gradually to our
senses. We all shot out of bed, feeling for our dressing
gowns in the dark shadows of the bedroom.

The first thing Gan did was to fling open the curtains.
White moonlight flooded the room together with the
bright lights of flares being dropped by the bombers. We
huddled together on Mum's and Gan's bed, at first too
stunned by the sheer din to utter a word.

Gan was the first to pull herself together. "This one's
on Devonport." She had to raise her voice to make
herself heard. "They're after the Dockyard again." Her
voice broke our dazed silence and six-years-old Jill
began to whimper. Mum drew Jill's head into the
muffling folds of her dressing gown.

For once, Sir Percy was unable to stiffen our
backbones. Sitting next to Gan I heard her invoke him,
but I don't think any one else did. So his demands that

we be brave and not let the League down were ineffective. I could feel Diane pressing close to me, feel her warmth through our thin dressing gowns, and a trembling I wasn't sure was hers or mine.

The gunfire became heavier but, as Gan shouted in our ears, it was our own. "It will be from the ships in the harbour," she told us and from the incessant clamour in our ears, she must have been right.

Above the din we heard a new sound, and Mum lost her nerve.

It was the first time we children had seen fear betrayed by an adult, and for us it was more traumatic than the raid itself. We heard a stick of bombs approaching us, the shrill whistle as one came down right above us, and Mum cried out, her voice cracked with fear, "Oh Mum, this is it."

I can't remember hearing the explosion when the bomb landed several streets away. Overriding everything was Gan's reaction. She shouted at Mum, "Of course it's not, you silly little blighter. Don't let me hear such tommyrot." The shock of hearing her berate Mum as she frequently did us, drove everything else from my mind.

The raid was sharp but mercifully short, unlike the earlier ones which had often lasted hours through the night. And that was the last raid we experienced from a ring-side seat. Under the stairs to the Shipleys' flat was a cupboard big enough for the five of us, and also for Mrs Shipley and Peter when they later joined us. As Gan said, in her "I give up" voice, "I always feel better if I can see what's going on, but it doesn't seem to work for the rest of you."

When Diane and I came home from school the next day, we were surprised to find Mrs Crisp in our kitchen, sharing a cup of tea with Gan. "Well, Henry's always out if there's a raid," Mrs Crisp was saying. "But last night it was worse knowing Connie was in Plymouth." Connie was the Crisps' A.T.S. daughter. Mrs Shipley had told us that Connie had been posted to Plymouth, though at the time Gan had refused to show any interest because of her row with Mrs Crisp.

Now she was full of sympathy. "But she's alright, isn't she?"

Mrs Crisp sighed. "Oh yes, thank God. But it was awful last night, worrying about her as well as Henry."

"Well, next time you're on your own, come to us," Gan said firmly. She poured another cup of tea, briefly glancing at Diane and me to remind us to hang up our coats. "What was your husband doing, did you know?" she asked.

"He was out fire-watching." Mrs Crisp sounded slightly vexed. "That's supposed to be a Civil Defence job, but the Home Guard have been asked to help out . . . though it's been emphasized that their main role is still to fight for their towns and villages if need be. And that's what Henry joined the Home Guard for, after all."

"Yes, but it's not likely we'll be invaded now, is it?"

"You never know," said Mrs Crisp sharply. "Just look at the raid we had last night. We all thought they were coming to an end, didn't we? You don't know what those Nazis are planning."

"If you ask me, the Nazis are more frightened of being invaded by us now," Gan said. "That's why we're being raided again . . . because they've found out about all these foreign troops massing here."

"I still think it's a cheek, giving the Home Guard fire-watching duties. There are too many getting out of it. Did you read about that man in Devonport who thought he shouldn't have to do it because he's over sixty? He signed the register, then went off to the pub. He's been fined, and serve him right! My Henry's not far off sixty, but he would never shirk his duty."

Gan's attempt to placate wasn't too successful. "Well, they'll be standing down the Home Guard soon, surely," she smiled. "There's no need for them now."

"That's where you're wrong, Mrs Cooper," snapped Mrs Crisp. "They've just had a Lt. Colonel talking to them and he says the Home Guard is as important as ever they were, even with invasion fears over. He says there is to be no letting up on Home Guard discipline or it could produce a snowball effect and the whole edifice could crumble."

Gan had begun to look sceptical. I didn't wait to hear any more. I went to the bedroom to look for Jill, thinking how quickly Gan and Mrs Crisp seemed to be falling out again. Though of course, I didn't know how long they had been working up to it before Diane and I came home.

Gan seemed to be running out of verbal opponents. Mrs Shipley had become difficult to pick a quarrel with, since she had developed an apparent determination not to let anything Gan said offend her.

Even when Gan told her about the Portman Pudding recipe being another name for Carrot Cookies, it failed to annoy her. Mrs Shipley merely said cheerfully, "Oh, I know Mrs Cooper. It's the same with Savoury Pancakes. They're nothing but glorified Bubble-and-Squeak, but at least they look more attractive for not being just thrown into the frying pan in one solid lump." She seemed quite oblivious of Gan's stiffening back at the implied criticism of one of her favourite recipes, but had gone on chattily, "He (Lord Woolton) hopes we'll fall for anything, as long as it's got carrots and potatoes in it."

Mum had little to say about Sam, and refused to be drawn when Gan's reading of her tea-leaves always seemed to carry a "Sam's Mother warning". And we all guessed she was at odds with her sister following our visit to Nottingham, when she received a letter a little less than friendly and remarked acidly, "Well, your Aunt Ida obviously didn't like it when I mentioned about the bombed house."

At Mum's puzzled expression she snapped, "I told her, she needn't have bothered taking us to see one bombed house, when we've got hundreds of them here."

That left Mrs Proctor, and I provided her with another opportunity to fall out with my cookery teacher, albeit from a distance. This time, it was nothing to do with my cooking ingredients. Mrs Proctor had given us a talk on how people can get used to eating anything, even something they would normally consider obnoxious, when they are desperate. As usual, when I got hold of fascinating information, I could not resist passing it on.

I repeated the tale about the Italians eating cats, which Gan already knew. "And the Poles are eating rats," I told her, at which she shuddered and said, "Yes, they probably are, poor souls."

It was when I told her about some recipes Mrs Proctor had seen in a women's magazine, that Gan hit the roof.

"I don't believe it," she exclaimed. "Squirrels and hedgehogs? The woman's barmy."

"It's true," I insisted. "She says they are delicious."

"Has she tried them?" Gan demanded.

"No, but she says if she was hungry enough she probably would . . . we all would."

"Nobody British would eat a squirrel."

"She's making it up, I tell you. Nobody British would eat a squirrel. And as for a hedgehog — how would you get rid of all the prickles?"

I began to explain. "There's a special way of cooking them. You . . . " but she would not let me finish.

"I've never heard of anything so ridiculous in all my life. If that's all she can teach you, she's wasting her time. She'd better go to Italy and teach them how to cook the cats."

"It would only be if we were starving," I said. "She didn't mean . . ."

But Gan's patience was at an end. "Oh, for Heaven's sake, Betty, shut up and finish peeling these potatoes."

Gan was so irritable and hard to please as 1943 drew to an end, the rest of us began to sink into despondency. Jill, always a quiet little girl, grew even more silent and crept round the house like a secretive mouse. Diane and I hardly dared speak to one another in Gan's hearing, always conscious of her brooding presence. Even Mum came home from work wary, as well as weary, without even one of Debbie's ribald stories to rouse Gan's sense of humour.

It would soon be Christmas, and none of us expected a joyful one. But we had reckoned without the joint efforts of Sir Percy and the Minister of Fuel and Power.

Shortages of fuel were so acute, the Government appealed to people to conserve it. All sorts of ideas were promoted, and one was to share a fire and cooking with a neighbour.

Gan said, though without any real enthusiasm, "I suppose we could invite the Shipleys down for

Christmas evening. We do owe them a visit." She was setting out Mum's evening meal, dropping lumps of potato into a thin Oxo gravy, splattering it over the slice of corned beef and carrot pie.

Without a word, Mum got up from the table and picked up her special pad and pencil from the sideboard. She scribbled backwards and forwards across the pad, filling up one page and starting another, while we all watched her with rising hope.

The message started as it always did. "Sir Percy says," Mum said quite seriously, " 'Just what I would expect from you, m'dear. It takes courage to put on a show when there's little to do it with and you almost feel too tired to make the effort.' "

She turned the page and scribbled some more. "He says, 'Make it a Christmas your guests will never forget, m'dear. Remember, you're a member of the League, and they all expect great things from you.' "

And that was what they got. Gan rose to the occasion that Christmas as she never had before, so that none of us (except Jill, who was too young) ever forgot it.

Mr Shipley could not be home for the holiday, so his wife and son went up to London to see him, the weekend before. When they came home they brought his elderly father, a widower, with them.

Both Mum and Gan worked hard in the kitchen on Christmas Eve. We children were allowed to watch for a short while but Gan could not endure us under her feet for too long, and Diane and I were given the job of taking Jill and ourselves for a walk. Diane buttoned Jill into her coat while I tied her shoelaces, listening to Gan telling Mum, "It says brandy, but you can use this blackberry wine, and we'll have to use soya flour instead of ground almonds." She lifted a slab of pastry out of the huge earthenware bowl, and picked up the rolling pin.

We came home to the wonderful smell of sausage rolls, cooling on the wire rack. Mum was doling spoonfuls of carrot jam into pastry cases and Gan was replenishing their empty wine glasses, to a hearty accompaniment of "Roll Out the Barrel".

Her voice petered out on a high note. "Now's the time to roll . . .", was as far as she got as we walked into the kitchen, by the look on her face sooner than she had hoped. Mum said hurriedly, "Go and sit by the window, there's good girls. Get a book out."

And Gan relented enough to give us a sausage roll each. She said, "They're called surprise sausage rolls," which prepared us for something out of the ordinary and they were. Each roll of satisfyingly thick pastry had a small plug of sausage at each end and was filled in between with slices of apple.

I can't remember what we had for Christmas dinner the next day. It was overshadowed by the excitement of preparing for our guests. The fire was lit in the front room . . . I don't think it had ever been lit before . . . after the heavy blackout curtains had been drawn across the window.

Diane and I had new red tartan dresses, which Mum had made, and Jill wore her new blue dress sent by Auntie Thelma from America, for her birthday. By the time the Shipleys came down, the room was warm and cosy, with soft light from our old oil-lamp, instead of electric light.

Gan could be a very good hostess when she wished to be. Peter was encouraged to play dominoes on the floor with us, while Mum and Mrs Shipley settled on the sofa together to talk about our new dresses and Mrs Shipley's renovated one.

"You'd never guess this band in the skirt was from two dusters, would you?" said Mrs Shipley proudly, and Mum earnestly assured her she wouldn't.

But the main reason for the evening's success was the instant rapport between Gan and Mr Shipley. They chatted together like old friends. As fast as the old man lavished praise on all she offered, so Gan piled more food and wine onto him. Both grew more mellow as the evening progressed, their faces glowing rosy red in the firelight, until Mr Shipley asked if he might take off his coat and Gan heartily urged him to make himself feel at home.

All Mum and Gan's hard work was a huge success, but Gan's Marzipan Potatoes were a tour-de-force. Mrs Shipley bit into one and said appreciatively, "Well, you'd never guess there were potatoes in these, Mrs Cooper."

Gan was triumphant. "Because there aren't," she chuckled. "It's a recipe from my old book, and you don't even have to cook them. I've a good mind to send Lord Woolton a copy — a potato recipe with no potato!"

It was nearly our bedtime and Mr Shipley offered to read us a story from a book he had brought with him. So the adults pulled their chairs closer to his and we

We sat at his feet to listen to the tale of
"The Monkey's Paw."

children sat at his feet, to listen to W. W. Jacobs's tale
of "The Monkey's Paw".

I can still feel the atmosphere in that firelit room, the
absolute silence except for the old man's quiet voice, as
he unfolded the eerie tale. I was spellbound, lost in the
hopes and fears of the old man and woman until, right
at the end of the story, when the woman waited for a
knock on the door and we did not know what would
confront her . . . Mr Shipley gave a loud rap on the
wooden arm of his chair and we leapt in fright.

We all drank toasts at the end, in Gan's sloe wine. Jill was promoted from milked, to watered wine, to join Peter. Diane and I drank it neat for the first time, which was probably why I did not have a nightmare that night, but slept as soundly as everyone else.

CHAPTER
FOURTEEN

"This case is about the most trumpery and rotten that the Ministry has brought for a long time . . . and that is saying something!"

(Defending Solicitor about the Ministry of Food's prosecution of a man for illegal trafficking in rabbits.)

More and more people seemed to know somebody who had been "taken to Court" for some minor offence. At first declaring it served all of them right, Gan began to change her views, though she continued to have little sympathy with thieves.

A soldier had been fined £1 in Torpoint for stealing a cycle lamp, always difficult to get hold of, and Gan had agreed with the Chairman of the Bench that it was "a mean, dirty trick". But she was aghast at a tale Mum brought home from Debbie, who knew a man who had been given six months hard labour for stealing a coat from an air-raid shelter. "Whatever would they have done if they'd caught that blighter who pinched all our washing," she exclaimed. "Shoot him?"

Most of the offences concerned food. Sam told Mum of more thefts from his farm but Gan perversely refused to sympathise with him or his mother, or a fellow farmer who had been fined one hundred guineas for illegally slaughtering two pigs. "He said they were rheumatic," Mum told her, and Gan burst into derisive laughter. "So that's what he was doing — putting them out of their misery!"

Gan had an entirely different opinion of rabbit offences, though her affinity was with the poachers rather than traders. A local man was fined £1 for trapping rabbits and Gan was indignant, if illogical.

"When I think how many Greg must have poached in Millbrook, and we were always thankful for them. And now here he is, fighting for his country, and those miserable devils would fine him if they got the chance!"

She was more scathing over a newspaper report of a Plymouth woman who was fined £1 for selling a rabbit at 1/7d a pound, instead of the controlled price of 11d. "And she had the nerve to say she thought that was for the rabbit before it was skinned," she said in disbelief. "1/7d a pound! And we used to get a whole rabbit from Greg for 6d."

Gan was not alone in considering many of the Ministry of Food's prosecutions as mean-minded, and more and more local offenders were successfully defended in the Magistrates' Courts.

Sometimes, the offender himself would put up such a spirited defence, as to draw the country people's admiration.

A Cornishman, the manager of a canteen, was charged with selling sweets without coupons. His defence was that the sweets, which he had sold to soldiers, were made out of the sweepings of sugar in the canteen. He said he should be praised rather than condemned, for sweeping the sugar off the floor, boiling it, skimming the dirt from it, then making it into fudge.

148

Make tea-leaf parcels and save coal for tanks . . .

The Chairman of the Bench convicted him, fining him £5. So he picked up the exhibit of sweepings, went outside and threw it over the police inspector's car. He was then charged with wasting food but argued that he could not waste food that was already wasted.

The conviction against him was later quashed on appeal, but the Chairman made him pay the costs as "he had given everyone a lot of trouble."

The fuel shortage became so acute, people had to guard against their coal being stolen, and at the same time, were bombarded with advice on how to make it go further.

There were often conflicting claims for people's waste. Women's magazines were full of good ideas. "Throw potato peelings on your fire, to give a warm, clear flame", urged one, while the Ministry of Food

149

wanted them for feeding pigs. "Make parcels of your tea-leaves with newspaper and save coal for tanks," ran a newspaper column, but at the same time the Ministry of Supply said they needed six newspapers with which to make every four cartridge boxes.

Old tea-leaves in particular, seemed a most versatile resource. Not only could they be made into tea-leaf parcels but if mixed with coal-dust and clay would make excellent fire briquettes. Another magazine journalist wrote, "Dry your tea-leaves, mix them, a quarter to three-quarters of tobacco to roll into your own cigarettes, and you will hardly be able to tell the difference".

The only people who did not want them were those at the Ministry of Food. "You can put practically anything into the pig-bin", they told us. "But not tea-leaves, or you will poison the pigs".

We continued to gather wood and anything else that would burn, along the shore-line near the Ferry. Many others did the same, though we never saw old Margy again. She had probably moved on.

Often the wood and cork we brought home was salt-saturated, or covered with tar, which caused the fire to spit as it ignited.

Gan took Jill shopping one day after we had come home from school, leaving Diane and me at home with the stern admonition to read quietly and keep out of mischief. She was hardly out of the door before we disobeyed her.

Temptation lay in a box in the bedroom, in which Mum kept her small treasures. Nothing in the box was valuable, but we found the contents fascinating. She

She highlighted her cheekbones to a gloriously hectic flush
and pouted the bright red lipstick into her lips.

had ear-rings made from pretty buttons and fuse wire, a
shell necklace and another made with nuts. There were
bits of make-up including several worn-down lipsticks,
a pot each of rouge and mascara, creams and
face-powder, a small phial of scent and a pair of
eyebrow tweezers. Diane and I had delved into this box
before, and were longing to get at it again.

Diane made straight for the rouge and lipstick. She
stared earnestly into Mum's small hand-mirror,
highlighting her cheek-bones to a gloriously hectic
flush, rubbing and pouting the bright red lipstick into
her lips as she had seen Mum do. We both thought she
looked beautiful.

"Let me do your eyebrows," I suggested, and though
she was reluctant after I had yanked out the first two or

three hairs, I got better at it, so quick that she did not feel a thing. I finished one eyebrow, then started on the other.

The trouble was, getting them to match. No matter how many hairs I pulled first from one and then the other, they did not look right. I began to feel alarmed and hastily told Diane, "It's my turn now. You try on the ear-rings while I do my face." I put on foundation cream, covered it over with face-powder and chose a dramatic, purply lipstick. We always had enough sense to leave the scent alone and I now knew we should have done the same with the tweezers.

Diane's anguished howl, when she looked in the mirror and saw what I had done to her eyebrows, changed into a horror-stricken wail. "What will Gan say," she cried. "She'll know what we've been doing."

We had just a few moments of paralysing panic, before something even worse came to galvanize us into action. Behind Diane's head, I saw a puff of smoke drift gently through the open bedroom door.

I rushed into the kitchen, my cry of "The fire!" bringing Diane charging after me. There on the fire-guard were the clothes Gan had left drying, flames leaping from them through billowing black smoke.

Again we were hit by panic. Without even having the sense to throw water over the blazing jumpers and stockings, we tore upstairs to fetch Mrs Shipley.

She came instantly, taking control. She snatched up a wooden spoon from the table, to hook up a burning stocking from the hearth-rug, before knocking the rest of the clothes from the fire-guard into the hearth.

152

"Go and get a bucket of water, Betty," she ordered me. "And Diane, move that towel before it catches."

When everything was safe, Mrs Shipley looked at Diane and me. We were both in tears. She said gently, "If I were you I'd go and clean off that make-up before your Gran sees you." We sped to the sink to do as she suggested, then lifted our faces for her inspection. She smoothed Diane's eyebrows with a sooty finger and waited with us until Gan and Jill came home.

"You've got two good girls here," she called, as soon as Gan's startled face appeared round the door. "The house might have been burned down if they hadn't been so sensible. It isn't often you can count on kids to do the right thing when they're on their own."

With one swift, all encompassing glance, Gan took in our guilty faces, the heap of smouldering clothes in the grate and the smoke-blackened wall beside it. I could not read her expression but did not expect to. Gan never betrayed anger with us in front of outsiders, which made waiting until they had gone all the more unnerving. She thanked Mrs Shipley profusely. "And I'd only slipped out for some bread," she declared. "It's tarred wood we'd picked up from the beach, it spits like an angry cat. Thank Heaven you were here. Will you stop and have a cup of tea with us?"

"No, I'll leave you to clear up the mess," said Mrs Shipley, sympathetically. She glanced at Diane and patted her downcast head. "This little one was very brave. She's singed off her eyebrows rescuing one of your towels."

I had a wild desire to cling to her, not to let her go, as she went out and left us with Gan. Gan said absolutely nothing for what seemed an age; she just stood and stared grimly at me. She then looked from me to Diane, who promptly burst into loud sobs and Gan's calm-before-the-storm was shattered.

"Oh, for goodness' sake, shut up," Gan shouted at Diane. "I haven't touched you yet." She glared back at me. "What the devil were you playing at, to let the fire get such a hold?"

I stammered, "W . . . we . . . we d . . . did . . . didn't know . . . what to . . . to do. We . . . left it and ran up . . . upstairs."

Gan was furious. "Trust you," she shouted at me. "Trust *you* to involve *her*! I can't leave you for a minute, without you letting the whole neighbourhood know our business." Her attention was drawn back to Diane, who hadn't the sense to stop howling. Jill had scurried to the window corner, keeping out of it.

"Stay where you are," Gan ordered Diane and stalked to the bedroom. She came back with Mum's tweezers.

"Keep still," she snapped, glaring into Diane's apprehensive face. "I'm not having your Mother seeing you looking like a half-scraped carrot." She pulled more hairs out of poor Diane's depleted eyebrows, finally giving up with an exasperated, "There, that's the best I can do! You'll have to wait now until they grow back."

I thought we had escaped very lightly, but I don't think Diane agreed.

154

Mum was sympathetic. "Don't worry about the stockings. We've no coupons for any more but we'll get some of this."

She showed us an advertisement in the paper for leg make-up. "Pour out eight pairs of stockings for 1s 3d" it said. She then produced a tin of Vaseline. "This will make your eyebrows grow faster," she assured Diane. "It makes eyelashes grow thicker too, and it's good for your hands."

Perhaps my interest as well as Diane's, made Mum realise we were growing up. She began to include us in her simple beauty treatments on Saturday nights.

We had face masks to improve our skin. We saved the shells when we had any fresh eggs, using the last little bit of egg-white as an astringent. When there were no eggs available, Fuller's Earth mixed with water made a deathly white mask, good for blackheads but bad when someone came to the door, because if you moved your face muscles the mask cracked. Vinegar made our hair shine while slices of cucumber brought a sparkle to our eyes. It was all fun and helped to foster a bond between us and Mum, which had not always been apparent.

CHAPTER
FIFTEEN

More than two-thirds of Cornwall has been designated a Prohibited Zone after 31/3/1944. People found in this Zone without authorisation will be liable for a £100 fine, or three months' imprisonment, or both. No-one is allowed to carry binoculars or a telescope.

(Western Evening Herald, April 1944)

Our family went through another fed-up period. As always, it stemmed from Gan's depression. Her mood, whether cheerful or miserable, always affected our lives even more drastically than the war events happening around us.

She got so low, Sir Percy suggested that we went to the pictures, even though it was only Thursday.

We went to see *Kitty*, a Pygmalion-type story, and it proved so therapeutic that we went to see it again on Friday and on Saturday.

The girl in the pay kiosk greeted us like old friends. "It must be a good film," she grinned but although Mum, Diane and I felt slightly silly, Gan rose to the occasion.

She patted Jill's head. "It's her birthday treat. She begged to come again." She smiled benignly down into Jill's wide eyes, my little sister's expression bemused

Gan got so low, Sir Percy suggested we went to the pictures, even though it was only Thursday.

between the surprise of hearing it was her birthday (it wasn't), and the discomfiture of having everyone staring at her.

We were early. The lights were still up on the noisily excited audience. The cinema was not yet full, though the back rows were already occupied with the usual sailors and their girls. Scattered around the rest of the cinema were a number of American soldiers, mostly in groups of three or four.

Our seats were several rows behind Emmy's two, on the end of the aisle. She was not there, which was unusual on a Saturday. There were very few seats left when the lights went down, to the joyous cheers and clapping of the audience.

We had been settled down about ten minutes, when a commotion started. The cause was immediately obvious. Emmy's large figure stood silhouetted between

157

us and the screen, and she was loudly berating the two unfortunate American G.Is who were sitting in her seats.

At first we could not hear what any of them were saying, although the people sitting alongside them were beginning to cast restive glances in their direction. We could see the nearest American put a soothing hand on Emmy's arm, which she immediately shook off. Then, in a quiet moment in the film the voice of the other American rose in frustration as he exhorted, "For crying out loud . . . take it easy, sister, will ya?"

Emmy's voice rose above Paulette Goddard's. She shouted, "I'm not your sister." She flared at the other man, "I'm not *your* sister," and turned to involve the people in the row behind. Excitement was mixing her up. "I'm not his sister," she told the woman behind her. "And he's not *my* sister."

By now, more people were getting agitated at the noise disrupting the film. I was on the end, aisle seat, about four directly behind Emmy, and I cowered down, horrified that she might look further back and enlist the support of her friends. Someone shouted, "Shut up, for Gawd's sake. Let those who want to, enjoy the film," to a chorus of agreement, while some of the other Americans in the audience, recognising their buddies were being got at, stood up and joined in. By the time the manager and an usherette came to sort things out, the audience was making more noise than the film.

The usherette coaxed Emmy to one side, though she refused to move more than a yard or two. The manager exchanged a few quiet words with the soldiers and they stood up. "Aw, come on, let's get out of here," said one

158

in disgust, while the other one seemed more disposed to listen to the apologetic manager's placatory words. They walked slowly past Emmy in calculated nonchalance and were joined at the top of the aisle by a number of their buddies, all loudly wanting to know, "What's going on around here?" before the manager succeeded in shunting all of them in the direction of his office. Emmy belligerently watched them go, her hands on her hips, before sashaying in triumph to her vacated seats.

Making our way out of the cinema when the programme was over, Gan asked the girl in the kiosk if she knew what had happened to the Americans.

"It's OK," the girl cheerfully assured her. "They understood about Emmy when the manager explained. And he's giving them complimentary tickets for next week, any day but Saturday."

One night, when Mum came home, Gan was agog with news.

"Guess who I met in the greengrocer's today! The Finchcombe's daughter, Iris."

At Mum's blank look she said, exasperated, "You know! The couple in the corner cottage in Millbrook."

Mum was nodding. "Yes, I remember. Iris and the children came to stay with her parents when they were bombed out. Are they still there?"

"No, they're in a flat the other side of Torpoint. But she had quite a bit of Millbrook news." Gan poured Mum a cup of tea. "Dinner's nearly ready," she said, and sat down with her own cup.

"Do you remember that houseboat we used to walk past, on the Lake? Well, there was a shooting there. A man living in the terrace up from the Lake, and he was taken to the police station to be charged with attempted murder. He's not someone we know, but Iris says her friend's sister lives next door to him."

Gan gulped the rest of her tea and went to the oven. She brought a well-browned cottage pie to the table and put a generous slice on Mum's plate.

"And Tom Dewey has been cautioned to keep the peace. It seems Miss Swithen rapped Effie on the knuckles for talking, and her Dad threatened to go up to the school and roll Miss Swithen down Blindwell Hill." Gan surrounded Mum's pie with carrots. "Of course, he would never have done it," she said scornfully. "He always was all talk."

"Any news about Tilda?" Mum asked.

"Yes, Greg's been home on leave and she's been walking him round the village, as pleased as Punch. Iris says he was sorry we'd left, because Tilda had told him how lonely she was after we had gone."

Gan and Mum exchanged speaking glances before Gan went on, "And they've been having a lot of trouble with people showing lights on Whitsands. They say it's people from Plymouth, who thought it was all right because they were only using candles. Would you believe it! When I think of all the fuss old Mr Brown made when he thought you hadn't camouflaged your torch enough. I bet he had a few words to say! Anyway, P.C. Polworthy now has to patrol the cliffs every weekend, and they were all fined, including the owners of the chalets."

Mum, too, had some news. "Debbie's husband is coming home on leave. She can't stop talking about it." She chuckled, "You wouldn't believe some of the things she's planning for their first night," then looked across the table to where I was sitting, interested in their conversation.

Gan followed her glance and glared at me. With no longer a secret language to resort to, no cat to send us to search for, all the shops closed and Diane and I, at twelve and thirteen, too old to have in bed before Mum came home from work, she was in a quandary. But not for long.

She snapped, "Go and fill the coal bucket, Betty. And make sure you fill it right to the top." Resignedly, I stood up, glancing at Diane and Jill. They were absorbed in a game of Cat's Cradle. Diane was never inquisitive like me.

When I came back, of course all the intriguing talk had ended. Mum was saying, a little defiantly, "Well anyway, whatever she gets up to, good luck to her. Heaven knows when she'll see him again. And all the girls are helping her out. Norma's giving her a jar of Oil of Arabia. Edith's got a bottle of Californian Poppy for her and Dora says she can borrow her see-through black nightie, the one she got from her American friend. I'll have to think of something."

Gan said shortly, "If I were you, I'd tell her to keep off the see-through black nightie. He might be suspicious as to how she came by it. You can give her a bottle of my damson wine, and tell her, if she gives him a couple of glasses of that, he won't be put off even if she's buttoned up to her ears in winceyette."

Jill was still awake when Diane and I went to bed that night, though at first we didn't realise it. As we were getting into bed in the dark, I whispered to Diane, "So what were Mum and Gan on about, when Gan sent me out to the coalhouse?"

Though I could barely see her face, I could tell Diane was surprised. "Don't know," she whispered back. "I wasn't listening."

A voice came out of the darkness, from Jill's little truckle bed. She had quite a deep voice for such a small girl. "Africa Dizzyax," she said, with all the importance of expounding unfamiliar words. "That's what they were talking about."

Diane and I sat up in bed, silently digesting this unexpected information. "Africa Dizzyax?" Diane repeated. "Who's going there?"

"Don't know," Jill said sleepily, and snuggled back down under her blanket.

There were a number of important visitors in Plymouth. General Eisenhower came to inspect the U.S. Army units, training for the invasion of Europe. Churchill and Montgomery also came. Mum was inspected by Monty, together with her fellow women workers in Devonport Dockyard and was given a pep talk stressing the importance of their work, but the thing she remembered most about him was how small he was.

162

The thing she remembered most about him,
was how small he was.

It was obvious to everyone that an invasion of Europe was imminent. For some time, movement in the South and West had been restricted, with no-one being able to visit coastal areas without permits, unless they lived there. More and more, people were stopped by the Army or Home Guard and asked to produce identity cards. We were stopped once, on one of our regular walks past Borough gun-site, two miles outside Torpoint, and another time on our way down to Wilcove, where ships lay at anchor.

There was a sudden shortage of vegetables, which hit us severely, as most of our meals were practically vegetarian. Gan was incensed. "What do they think they're playing at?" she wanted to know. "We're surrounded by fields full of cabbages and potatoes, yet the greengrocer has run out." So she led us, like Fagin, to a farmer's field at Borough, not far from Torpoint, and for the first and only time in our lives, Diane and I were sent to steal.

At first, it all seemed quite exciting, going out in the early dusk to forage. It reminded us of our old wood-gathering expeditions along the country lanes outside Millbrook, only with an added element of risk.

It was a different matter when we arrived at the vegetable fields beyond Borough. Diane was suddenly stricken with horror that someone ... anyone ... would see her. She emerged from the field clutching a cabbage, to thrust it with trembling hands into Gan's bag, before we made our way to the turnip field.

It was my turn now. Like Diane, I had had time to think, only my fear was more specific than hers. What if a soldier suddenly appeared, and asked me for my identity card?

While not being particularly brave, I always had a streak of bravado in me ... Gan called it showing off. I walked boldly to the nearest turnip, grabbed it up and brought it back to Gan, my heart thumping so loudly it was a wonder she didn't hear it and tell me to shut it up.

That was our last vegetable forage. Gan would never have got Diane to do it again, and my effort was entirely wasted when Gan found out that my turnip was a mangel wurzel, fit only for cattle food.

A week or so after Emmy's skirmish with the American soldiers, we witnessed another incident over

164

her broken-down cinema seats, though this time she was not there.

Halfway through the film, it broke down. This often happened and, as usual, the audience became restive, catcalling, whistling, thumping their feet and waving their arms.

There was a young couple sitting in Emmy's seats, the man waving his arms as enthusiastically as any one, when he flung himself hard back against his seat and it broke away. He went sprawling into the aisle with a yell, causing even more agitation among the people around him.

"What a good job poor old Emmy wasn't sitting there," Gan remarked, as the young man and his indignant girlfriend were directed to other seats by the usherette. "She might have done herself some real damage."

CHAPTER
SIXTEEN

"There were Rats, Rats, Big as Bloomin' Cats"

(From the song "Quartermaster's Store")

Food shortages became so acute, Gan's wasn't the only temper with a shortened fuse. Mrs Shipley, normally a very even-tempered young woman, had a row with a woman in front of her in a lemon queue.

She had gone to Plymouth in response to a newspaper article announcing the arrival of a consignment of lemons, and joined a long queue outside a city greengrocer. She was very incensed, telling the tale to Gan.

"Would you believe anyone would have the nerve," she demanded. "There was this woman, walked up to the woman in front of me, and greeted her like a long-lost friend. And then, the crafty madam, she kept moving up with the queue, and there was a whole lot of chuntering going on behind me. So when we got as far as the shop door, I said, 'Excuse me, but I think you've jumped the queue.' Well! She gave me a mouthful, I can tell you but then all the women behind joined in and stuck up for me. So she had no choice. She went flouncing off to the back of the queue, bold as brass. And the woman she had cottoned on to reckoned she

She didn't know what was round the corner,
but hoped it was onions.

didn't know her, that she'd thought it was just a case of mistaken identity!"

Gan was warm in her praise. "I'm glad you spoke up," she said. "Too many people get away with queue-jumping, if they're hard-faced enough."

Gan had no interest in lemons. Her abiding longing was for onions and Mum often spent her lunchtime trying to get some. There was a greengrocer in Devonport, near the Dockyard, where a rumour of the arrival of anything in scarce supply was enough to draw a queue half way round the block. Mum more than once joined on the end of it, without knowing what was round the corner, but hoping it was onions.

Later that week, we met Mrs Shipley in the passage. She was chuckling. "Guess what, Mrs Cooper? I won the first prize in the raffle at the Make-do-and-Mend Group last night . . . and it was a lemon!"

Obsession with food shortages showed itself in another way. There was an appeal in the local paper, asking every man, woman and child to become a rat reporter. We were told that two million tons of food were being eaten every year by forty million rats, and that there were almost as many rats as people. People were asked to report any stray rats they saw so that experts could follow them home to their colonies, which often contained one thousand rats, and destroy them. We were told to ask for the Rat Officer.

Mrs Proctor, our cookery teacher, gave us a pep talk about rats, telling us it was our duty to keep a lookout for them. There were extensive cellars underneath the old Cookery School, not far from the water's edge, and the more stout-hearted of her pupils (which did not include me), used to go in there at playtime and come out swearing they had seen rats' eyes gleaming in the dark.

Gan, of course, didn't agree with Mrs Proctor's attempts to turn us into rat hunters. "Rat hunts?" she snorted. "It's a wonder she doesn't want you to take one in for a pie." She thrust a knife into my hand. "Just you leave the rats alone and get on with those carrots."

It was my thirteenth birthday in April. A week earlier, a parcel of clothes had arrived from Auntie Thelma in America and I was allowed to choose a dress from it. The one I chose was full length, made in green and white seersucker with a zip down to the knees, and I thought it was heavenly. For a long time I refused to have the bottom cut off it, and floated round the kitchen in it until Gan had had enough. "For Heaven's sake," she exclaimed at last, exasperated. "Stop parading around like Lady Muck." So it was cut shorter to make a summer dress for me, and Mum must have left plenty to make a big hem, because I was still wearing it when I was eighteen.

One of my presents was a silver cross and chain from Sam. We seldom saw him now, though Mum and he still went out together some weekends.

But the best part of my birthday was a family party to the Forum in Devonport. We had postponed it until the end of the month, to see a film of my favourite cowboy, Roy Rogers, and his horse, Trigger. Mum was working at the Dockyard that morning, and we met her outside the cinema.

Gan had filled a large biscuit tin with an assortment of sandwiches which she said was to be a lucky dip. It was a glorious mixture. Sitting in the darkened cinema, you didn't know until you bit into a sandwich whether it would be sardine or jam, dried egg mixed with chopped onions or proper egg, the ones with yolk and white. There were some filled with condensed milk or soft brown sugar and Jill was sure she got a mushy peas one, though Gan would not admit to anything specific. "It's half the fun to guess," she insisted, and it was. We had a walk round Devonport Park when we came out of the Forum and went home on the ferry, tired and happy.

We were woken abruptly in the middle of that night by pandemonium. The siren was wailing, we could already hear aircraft overhead, and Gan had stubbed her toe on the wheel of Jill's bed as she flung her feet to the floor. In such a confined space, in the dark, there was bound to be chaos, though we all knew exactly where to feel for our clothes and shoes. Mum hauled

Jill out of her bed and Gan was hustling Diane and me out of the door while Diane was still struggling to get her second arm into her dressing gown.

After the bad raid at the end of 1943 it had been agreed we would go under the stairs in future. "Get in the cupboard, quickly," Gan ordered. "There's a torch in there, but don't put it on until we're all in, with the door closed."

We heard Mrs Shipley and Peter clattering down the stairs and Gan called out to them, "If you don't fancy the shelter, there's plenty of room for all of us under the stairs. I'll bring some pillows for us to sit on."

So Diane, Peter and I crept to the far end of the cupboard, our heads bent to our knees where the staircase met the floor, and everybody else packed in behind us.

The crescendo of noise was rising outside, as the inevitable explosions and gunfire followed, but as Gan squeezed herself in with a pile of pillows in her arms, she closed the door behind her and with it, much of the frightening din.

I passed the torch to Mum, who shone it around our closely huddled figures, while Gan shared out the pillows. Eerie looking faces peered out of the shadows, picked out one at a time by the torchlight. Mrs Shipley began to laugh, though a little breathlessly. "Peter, you look like an evil little gnome," she teased him, so Peter played up to his image, pulling faces while Mum shone the torch under his chin, making everyone laugh.

Very quickly, Gan began to organise singing and poem reciting. A little more sensitive as I grew up, I had

170

lost my earlier complacency that everyone wanted to hear me recite from my large repertoire of epic poems, every time there was an air-raid. I tried to make excuses. "I'm too crouched over to recite," I pleaded, but Gan was adamant. "I'm sure Mrs Shipley would like to hear 'Lochinvar'," she insisted, and of course Mrs Shipley said, yes she would.

So once again I recited my show-piece, the poem I would for ever afterwards associate with air-raids. For an encore I began "The Noble Boy". I had just got to the saddest bit, where the old woman stood "alone, uncared for, amidst the throng", reciting it in a suitably doleful voice, when we heard the land-mine.

It was a heavier, duller explosion than the H.E.s we were used to hearing. It shook the house and cut me off in mid-sentence.

Gan, of course, knew instantly what it was. "But it's no worse than an ordinary bomb," she declared. "Just a bit bigger, that's all." For the first time ever, she let me get away with an unfinished recitation.

"Well, that's enough of being mournful," she said firmly. "Now let's have 'Roll out the Barrel', and see who can sing the loudest."

As we sang, Peter started clambering over Diane's legs, drawing a loud yelp from her, to reach his mother and whisper urgently in her ear.

"Sorry, Mrs Cooper, I'll have to get past you," she apologised. "Peter needs to go." So Gan opened the cupboard door, letting the deafening noise in, though with her acute hearing, she was still able to hear Jill's tentative, "Mum . . .!" and to interrupt her with a firm "No, you don't Jill".

We sat silently waiting for the Shipleys to come back. It was amazing how much braver we felt, when there was someone outside the family to share the danger.

Mrs Shipley brought Peter back together with a packet of chocolate biscuits. "Here, I think we all deserve one," she declared, handing them round. "And the raid seems to be getting further away. They've probably moved on to some other poor so . . . devils."

After the All Clear, Gan herded us all into our kitchen, switching on the bright, overhead light in the blackouted room. We all looked a mess in the hard light. Mrs Shipley did not look as attractive without her make-up and with the front bit of her hair in curlers. Mum looked tired, her face pale and puffy, and chocolate had melted into her cardigan sleeve, where Jill had temporarily lost her biscuit. Gan lacked some of her usual dignity. She had hair-wavers in, something she normally scorned any woman for being seen in, outside her own family. Heaven knows how she slept in them. They were like large bulldog clips and must have dug into her head as she lay on them, but she always used them when she washed her hair.

Gan poured cups of milk for all of us children, noting our weary faces. "Drink up," she said. "And off to bed, all of you. Your Mum, Mrs Shipley and I are going to have a cup of tea before we come."

Mrs Shipley put her arm round Peter, grimaced at his chocolate-coated mouth and hands and said, "Well, he's going straight into bed as he is, poor kid. I'm not waking him up with a cold flannel."

Jill was asleep almost as soon as she was tucked back into bed. Diane and I lay longer awake, whispering in the dark until we heard Gan calling goodnight to Mrs Shipley on the stairs.

Even after Mum and Gan had settled in bed, and Diane breathed evenly beside me, I could not get to sleep.

I tried to conjure up Roy Rogers and his white horse, the picnic in the cinema, the walk round the park before we caught the ferry, but it all seemed so much further away than yesterday afternoon. My last memory as I finally fell asleep was of the warm smell, the closeness, when seven people are crowded together in a broom cupboard.

We were lucky it was Sunday and we didn't have to go to school or work in the morning. Throughout the day, we got snippets of news about the night raid. Mrs Shipley came to tell us about the land-mine. "Mrs Crisp's just been in," she said. "Her husband's platoon was called out to clear up. It was dropped at Anthony Farm, just along the road, and it had a parachute on it."

Gan said, "I heard twenty cows were killed. Was that by the land-mine?" Mrs Shipley didn't know. "But Mrs Crisp thinks they were after all the ships gathering in the Sound and up the river, and of course she's right. They wouldn't have been aiming at poor old Farmer Pengelly, though I don't suppose that's any consolation to him."

"I heard one plane was brought down in the sea," Gan said and Mrs Shipley nodded. "Haven't found out where yet, though," she said. Gan had the satisfaction of finding out where, before Mrs Shipley. One evening, a few days after the raid, Mrs Finchcombe called. She had been to see her daughter Iris and had responded to Iris's earnest entreaty that Gan had said she would love to see her next time she came to Torpoint.

As soon as we heard the knock on the back door, Gan's hackles began to rise. "Whoever can it be?" she wondered crossly, always hating unexpected visitors. But when she saw her old neighbour from Millbrook, she made her very welcome.

The two women chatted happily over a cup of tea and one of the peanut brownies Mum always made when Auntie Thelma sent a jar of peanut butter. Mum, as always, was content to sit and listen.

Mrs Finchcombe knew all about the German plane which had come down in the sea.

"It came down off Whitsands," she said. "The crew escaped by parachute and they were captured by the Home Guard patrolling the cliffs, as they came ashore in rubber dinghies."

"Well, I don't know," Gan exclaimed. "For a tiny village, you do get some excitement. Do you remember the German airmen who parachuted down near Rame, and one of them fell into the sea off Cawsand? They were carted off to Millbrook Police Station. More tea, Mrs Finchcombe?"

"Thank you, Mrs Cooper." Mum, at a flick of the eye from Gan, got up to fetch the teapot off the stove.

174

"We had some bombs dropped at Cremyll, too."

"Is that where all those cows were killed?" asked Gan, but Mrs Finchcombe did not think so.

"Well, they were certainly after the shipping in the Sound," Gan said. "I bet you'll see a lot, from Cawsand."

"Yes, but you have to be careful how long you look," Mrs Finchcombe said. "Tilda Hawkins went for a walk there, with young Andy and do you know, she was stopped by a soldier and asked for her identity card and he told her she could be fined £100 and get three months in gaol for looking at ships."

"He was having her on," Gan said scornfully. Unexpectedly, Mum spoke. "No, it's true," she said. "It's since the ban on movement along the coast. They say two-thirds of Cornwall is affected by it."

He told her she could be fined £100 *and* get three months in gaol for looking at the ships.

"Yes, but surely no-one would suspect a young woman and a little boy," protested Mrs Finchcombe.

Gan drank some tea and put her cup down. "How is Tilda?" she asked. "Has Greg gone back?"

"Yes, poor girl. She says she feels so lonely without him. I've told her to come round to us whenever she wants, but she says she must carry on. I think she's very brave."

She finished her tea and stood up. "Mustn't be late getting back to Iris and the kids," she said. "I'm staying with her tonight." She looked kindly at Mum. "I bet you find it easier getting to the Dockyard from here, Ida. The 'Western Belle' is no joke, especially on a stormy night. Did you hear about Mrs Benson? You know, Hetty Pendennis's sister-in-law. She fell over a rope on the ferry, in the blackout. She hurt her eye, had to have three days in bed and a fortnight off work. She had to pay the doctor two guineas and they say she'll be scarred for life. She works in the Dockyard, in the canteen. Do you know her?" Mum shook her head. "She says she lost £10 in wages and food she would have had in the canteen. Anyway, she's got £88 damages . . . that's not bad is it? But it just shows how careful you have to be in the blackout."

Gan saw her out and came back, looking thoughtful. "Fancy that woman getting all that money for falling over a rope," she exclaimed. "From what I remember about her from Mrs Pendennis, she was as blind as a bat . . . couldn't see more than a yard or so, even with thick glasses. And then she had the nerve to blame the blackout."

Mum answered reasonably, "Well, what does it matter whether it was the blackout or her short-sightedness? They shouldn't have left a rope lying around."

"Of course it matters," Gan snapped. "She could hardly blame the boatmen for her poor sight."

"Or for the blackout," Mum said, but she was beginning to sound less confident. "But they should have been more careful where they . . ."

"Oh, have done," Gan roughly interrupted. "If I can't get it through to you . . . I give up."

Mum said no more. I must have reached the age of logic, because I could clearly see her point. Of course, I did not tell Gan.

CHAPTER
SEVENTEEN

"It is always the best policy to speak the truth unless, of course, you are an exceptionally good liar."

(Jerome K. Jerome)

Mum came home from work one evening, just as she always did, but we knew instantly that something was wrong. She came in, put down her bag and took off her coat, without a word. No expected smile for us, no quick cuddle for Jill, waiting near her chair, only a face stiff with sorrow.

Gan's usual ready account of some incident in her day, often begun before Mum had got her coat off, was forgotten. "Come and sit down, Ida," she said gently. "What is it?"

Mum sat at the table and said in a shaking voice, "Debbie's lost her husband. They fetched her to the office this morning and told her. He was on a mine-sweeper that hit a mine, and was not among those picked up."

The silence in our kitchen was deathly, as we shared Mum's grief for her friend. Though the rest of us had only met Debbie two or three times, we knew so much about her, she was a part of our lives. Mum had worked on the next machine to her, in the Dockyard, from the day she started work there over three years ago. She had come home with so many tales of the earthy, often vulgar but always humorous young woman, that Debbie stories had become a tonic, especially to Gan.

Gan said slowly, "To think, he was home on leave only a few weeks ago. Poor Debbie."

Mum was only just hanging on to her self control. She said, "They had a marvellous time. They . . ." then bit her lip.

Gan poured her a cup of tea, putting precious extra sugar in it. "Here, get this down you," she said gruffly. "And thank Heaven they had that leave for her to remember."

I looked at Mum. Her mouth was shaking even from between clenched teeth, and a sob rose in my throat which I could not stop. I burst into tears, as much for Mum's grief as sympathy for Debbie, and Mum immediately joined me.

Gan was not too patient with me. "Go into the bedroom and get a hanky," she told me sharply. "For Heaven's sake . . . your mother is upset enough without you making it worse."

So I rushed into the bedroom and cried for Mum and Debbie and her lost husband, and did not come back until my tears had dried up.

In that same week we heard of the death of another sailor. We did not know him and his death was not due to enemy activity, but his loss must have brought misery to someone. He had fallen off Torpoint Ferry in the dark and was last seen swimming away with a torch and shouting to his mates that he was alright. But he never reached the shore.

Hearing of this second tragedy made Gan, always superstitious, prophesy that we would soon hear of a third. If we did, I don't remember it.

My life at cookery school was becoming more and more difficult. I had told so many lies about Gan already, in my incessant efforts to avoid the embarrassment of never having the proper ingredients for my cooking, I was running out of plausible tales.

Mrs Proctor announced after one lesson, towards the end of the term, that she had something really exciting to tell us. We were to cook a dinner, and invite our teachers from school to eat it, and we would also act as waitresses to serve the meal.

Mrs Proctor said we had to ask our parents for a donation, in food and money. We were to bring two shillings and were each allocated some items of food. "And I'm counting on every one of you participating," she said, looking round our eager faces. "It will be a great opportunity for you."

My eager face was a complete sham. Behind it, my brain churned in anxiety. Would Gan even give me the one ounce of suet, two potatoes and a slice of corned beef, all to be brought on the day of the dinner, together with half a cup of red jam, which was to be my contribution, let alone two shillings?

She would not. She went through my list with her usual impatience, substituting most of the ingredients for something else. "Suet? It'll have to be lard. You can have the potatoes but I haven't any corned beef, and I won't have any next week either. And why does she want red jam? She can have some carrot jam and be thankful."

As I had feared, she was incensed about the two shillings. "Do you mean to tell me we're expected to pay for a meal for your teachers?" she demanded "They've got a nerve. It's them who should be paying, not us!"

In desperation, I said the worst thing I could have. I blurted out, "Mrs Proctor says we *must* bring the two shillings and the ingredients, or she might have to cancel it for everybody."

Gan's expression was so angry, I waited to hear no more than her furious, "Well, you can tell Madam Proctor from me . . ." before bolting outside to the lavatory to wait for her to simmer down. When I eventually crept back into the kitchen, casting her a nervous glance, I could see she was still seething. All she said, however, was, "We'll see about That Woman, and her old buck," but the way she said it filled me with foreboding.

On my next cookery lesson day, I didn't have to pretend to feel sick, the queasiness in my stomach was genuine. Of course, Gan didn't believe me.

She said sharply, "You were all right last night, when you ate those three baked potatoes. There's nothing wrong with you now." She pushed me out of the door with my potatoes, jam and lard, but with no money.

All the way to school my mind was feverishly engaged in thinking of a tale to tell Mrs Proctor. Should I say I had lost the money? That I had forgotten to ask Gan for it? Or say I could only pay it in instalments from my sixpence a week spending money? It never occurred to me to tell the truth, that Gan just would not give it to me, and none of these excuses seemed heart-rending enough. Once again, as so often before, my evil genius turned me away from a simple lie to an inventive, sympathy-seeking one.

I went to Mrs Proctor's table, where she was sitting with a note-book and money tin next to the register.

"We've just found out, Gan has to have an operation," I said. "All our money has to go to pay for it, even my spending money. I'm sorry about the two shillings, but it's urgent. She has to have it next week."

Mrs Proctor stared hard at me. "I'm sorry to hear that, Betty," she said. "I'll see what I can do from school funds."

There was one other girl who had not brought any money. Beryl Sweeney simply said flatly, "My Mum says I can't have it," and I was filled with admiration at her courage.

We had no cookery lesson that day, but a cleaning one. "Everything must be spick and span for our guests next week," Mrs Proctor told us. "And I want you to learn that scrubbing and washing up should be a pleasure, never a chore."

And it was, at least for me. Gan never wanted our help with cleaning at home. Not that we ever saw her do any . . . she must have done it while we were at school.

We had cleaned the pots and pans until they shone, scrubbed the boards white, and it was time to go home when I looked up and saw Gan standing at the classroom door with Jill.

My heart lurched, or was it my stomach that sank? Probably both. I was stunned to see her there, mortified that she had almost certainly come to have a row with my cookery teacher, in front of my classmates.

Mrs Proctor did not know who she was and called pleasantly, "Did you want to see me? If you wouldn't mind waiting until the girls are out."

I walked slowly towards Gan and she thrust a key into my hand. "Here, go home," she brusquely ordered me. "Diane won't be able to get in."

Thankfully, I scurried out with the other girls, unhappily aware of Mrs Proctor's surprised glance, from me to Gan.

I was too upset to answer Diane's surprised enquiries as to Gan's whereabouts. When Gan came home, half an hour later, pushing a shell-shocked looking Jill in front of her, she wasted no time. "Get into the bedroom," she said grimly to me. "I want a few words with you."

I don't think she knew where to begin. Breathing heavily, her wrathful eyes boring into mine, she finally demanded, "What have you got to say for yourself?"

Gan arrived home half an hour later, pushing a shell-shocked looking Jill in front of her.

I had nothing to say, beyond a mumbling "Sorry." I tried to keep out of her reach, but there was nowhere to retreat to.

"Why did you tell all those damned lies? Why?"

I just stared at her like a paralysed rabbit until she lost her temper and boxed my ears and I burst into loud sobs.

"And I should think so." Gan shouted at me. "All those lies about me having to have an operation, and us having no money. I could have sunk through the floor! I thought for one moment she was going to offer to help us out and I can tell you, if she had I'd have flattened her!" Sick with relief I realised that Mrs Proctor could not have got round to mentioning school funds.

"And all those tales you've come home with, about her being sickly. Why, I've never seen a better preserved woman. She must weigh twelve stone if she's an ounce. And I'm not surprised when I think of all our cheese rations she's had! Why did you do it? What was the idea?" Unable to tell her, I watched her dumbly, driving her to greater exasperation.

"Well, you can stay here and think about it," Gan said at last. "You can come out when you've got something to say for yourself."

So I stayed in the bedroom for the rest of the evening. Mum brought me something to eat before bedtime, but she was grave and did not say anything, so I expect Gan had told her everything.

It was Monday night, a miserable start to the week. I woke up the next morning with the depressing certainty

"I've never seen a better preserved woman. She must be twelve stone if she's an ounce!"

186

that Gan would not be speaking to me. Misdemeanours were never quickly forgotten. One as bad as this would probably chill the atmosphere for a week or more.

Gan was listening to the wireless when the three of us crept quietly into the kitchen. It was Diane who drew a rebuke. She began to speak but was instantly hushed.

"Ssshh," Gan hissed, so we sat silently at the table, where bowls of thick, steaming porridge waited for us. When she came to pour milk on to our bowls, her eyes were bright, her face animated.

"It's the invasion," she told us. "Our men have landed in France."

I have never forgotten the excitement of that moment. We had known for a long time that invasion was imminent. Although the soldiers, many of them Americans, had been hidden away in their camps, away from curious eyes and ears, it was impossible to conceal the increasing numbers of ships lying in and around Plymouth Sound, as the invasion fleet began to assemble.

I spoke up, more than a little tentatively. "Does that mean the war will soon be over?" I asked, and Gan answered me. "Yes, it's the beginning of the end," she exulted, and I knew immediately that the news was so marvellous, even my sins had become insignificant.

It was a fortnight later, before I saw Mrs Proctor again. Beryl and I had to stay in school on the teachers' dinner day. When I did see her, she was nicer to me than I had expected.

"Well Betty, I'm sure you won't tell untruths again." She was even too kind to call them lies. "They're not worth the mess they get you into, are they? Believe me, it's less trouble to tell the truth."

I remembered Miss Croft, my teacher in Millbrook who had been so concerned with my propensity for invention. She had always emphasised the immorality of it. Now older, growing up, Mrs Proctor's practical slant had an instant appeal for me. I knew she was right; my over-fertile imagination had always brought me nothing but trouble. I made a resolve to never tell another lie, and after D-Day, quite often I kept it.

CHAPTER
EIGHTEEN

"Good-bye-ee! Don't cry-ee!
There's a silver lining in the sky-ee."

(From a First World War song)

The euphoria over the invasion of Europe pervaded our house for weeks. We sat round the wireless, listening to the news bulletins pouring out of France, none of us daring to utter a sound as Gan hung on every word. People in the streets were filled with optimism, strangers more friendly to one another than they had been since Dunkirk. Local women took the increasing food shortages with determined cheerfulness. Gan even refused to grumble after standing in a butcher's queue for over half an hour for liver, and ending up with cow's heel.

One day Jill knocked a pan of boiled potatoes into the sink as she was reaching for a drink of water. She turned a frightened face to Gan while Diane and I winced in anticipation of an angry outburst. But all Gan said was, "Never mind," as she shovelled the potatoes back into the saucepan with a large spoon. "If this is all we have to put up with, we're lucky. Think of our boys in France and what they're going through." So we all thought of our boys in France as we ate our potatoes, and even Diane didn't pull a face at the

189

peculiar flavour which we could taste despite a liberal
drenching with Oxo gravy. She was lucky in not recognising
it. Unfortunately for me I had seen Gan empty a pail of
soapy suds down the sink, just before Jill's mishap.

Debbie's friend, Dora Shingle, had rushed to St.
Budeaux, to watch the Americans embark on their
landing craft, on their way to France, and was distraught
because she did not see her friend. "I'll never see him
again," she had wept in Debbie's arms and Debbie had
said to Mum, with a sigh, "I don't think she will either.
I always thought Hank had a married look about him."

"I always thought Hank had a married look about him."

"How he could have interfered with her
while he was driving the bus, I'll never know!"

Since losing her husband, the heart had gone out of Debbie, and with it the earthiness of her humour. But she still had many a tale to tell Mum, of her family and friends, and of friends of friends.

One light evening, as we got ready for a walk towards Borough to search for damsons, Mum said to Gan, "Do you remember that friend of Debbie's who caused a bus crash? She was a clippie on a double-decker."

Gan paused before asking, "Was she the one who was interfered with by the driver? Though how he could have interfered with her while he was driving the bus I'll never know."

"No," Mum explained. "It was her tickets he interfered with. And she was so angry with him she reached through the emergency hole and knocked his hat over his eyes."

"Yes, I remember," Gan said shortly. "She made him crash into a lamp-post, didn't she? And weren't some of the passengers hurt?"

"Yes, they were, and the top deck was badly damaged."

Gan said, her voice grim, "The stupid woman. Let's hope she gets a stiff sentence. She should have had more sense, no matter what he'd done."

"Well, she hasn't," Mum told her. "She's been fined a pound."

Gan was incredulous. "A pound? Surely not!" Mum's reply was emphatic. "A pound! Debbie says they were all flabbergasted that she got off so lightly."

Gan was so indignant, she was temporarily lost for words. She thrust a bag into each of Diane's and my hands then told Jill, "You can help your Mum," before bursting out with, "I don't know what this country's coming to! I was reading about some poor woman in the paper who's been sent to prison for three months for stealing a pair of shoes, yet here's this clippie gets fined a pound for nearly killing someone. Where's the justice in that?"

Gan very often got incensed over newspaper stories, though not always with the people they were about. She fell out with me once, merely for bringing one to her notice.

It all started off harmlessly enough with something Mum and Gan did fairly often. They went to consult a medium, this time a woman who practised in a quiet back street in Torpoint.

192

It was a Saturday afternoon and for once, Diane and I were left at home in charge of Jill, something Mum and Gan seldom did.

"Keep away from that fire," Mum warned. "And don't answer the door if anyone comes," added Gan. "Get on the floor and keep out of sight."

They were unusually quiet when they returned home. After taking off her coat, Gan stalked immediately to the teapot, while Mum smiled at us, but in a preoccupied way. They were obviously in the middle of an argument.

"If you ask me, she couldn't have made it plainer," Gan said tersely over her shoulder. "It was a warning to you, to get out of it while you can."

Mum got out two cups and poured in milk and added saccharins, before saying quietly, "All she warned me against was interference from an older woman."

"Exactly!" Gan brought the watered teapot to the table and glared at Mum. "So how could you be happy living with Sam if his mother is there interfering all the time? Your marriage wouldn't stand a chance. A mother of an only son always has the whip hand. Believe me, I had enough trouble with your dad's mother, and she wasn't even living with us."

Mum started to say, in a tight sort of voice, "Perhaps she didn't mean . . ." then paused before finishing. "They don't always get things right."

Gan exploded. "Well if that's what you think, what's the point in going?"

Mum said, "All I'm saying is" . . . then didn't say it.

193

At thirteen, I was growing out of a blindly defensive attitude in all my dealings with Gan, and developing a more positive desire to pour oil on troubled waters. While Mum and Gan were out I had read an account in the *Western Evening Herald* about a woman who had been charged under an eighteenth-century Witchcraft Act. Without really understanding its significance I seized on what I thought was a fascinating snippet, with which to divert Gan.

I said quickly, "There's a woman in yesterday's paper who has a Spirit Guide, just like you, Gan. Only hers is a Zulu instead of an Indian Sioux." We all knew about Red Feather, Gan's Spirit Guide, a strong, silent presence who stood at her right shoulder, unlike Sir Percy who was extremely articulate and always led from the front.

I had certainly diverted her, though the sharp glance directed at me wasn't as intrigued as I'd expected . . . more aggravated. But I knew she would be interested once she had read it. Anything to do with the Spirit World interested her. She snatched the paper from my hand and ran her eye down the column.

Because Gan did not say anything, I felt impelled to do so. "It sounds a bit like that place we went to in Devonport, doesn't it? Do you think it's the same woman?" Gan seemed so absorbed in the newspaper, I began to wonder if she was listening to me.

I went on chattily, "I know what conspiracy is, but what's conjuration?"

Her sudden angry outburst was completely unexpected.

Slapping the newspaper down onto the table so hard, it splashed tea out of her cup, she glared at me and demanded, "Just what are you getting at?" Her colour, already high because of her argument with Mum, alarmingly concentrated into two hectic patches over her cheekbones.

I could feel the cheerful smile still on my face. It had stuck there, like the joker's inane grin, goading her.

"So you think you're being funny, do you? I'll give you funny!" The sight of her furious face, closing on mine, galvanised my frozen muscles. I jumped up from the table, knocking some more of Gan's tea into her saucer and dragged my gaze from her to Mum. I must have looked aghast, because Mum came to my rescue, drawing Gan's fire to herself.

"For Heaven's sake, Mum," she said, more sharply than I had ever heard her speak to Gan. "You don't need to take it out on the kids."

Her response, so untypical of her normally conciliatory nature, petrified us all. Gan was as taken aback as the rest of us. Her face went a darker red, the colour spreading down her neck to somewhere underneath her wrathfully heaving blue jumper. She gave Mum a blazing glare then without another word she turned away from us all to march, stiff-backed, to the door. We heard the bedroom door slam behind her and knew we were in for one of her prolonged silences.

As always, when Gan fell out with us all, we did not dare talk freely to one another. Mum, her nerve gone, mouthed, "Find something quiet to do until tea-time, there's good girls." So while she sliced the bread, we played cards, though with "Snap", then "Old Maid", whispered instead of shouted, the games lacked sparkle.

This particular sulk of Gan's lasted a week, until Sir Percy had had enough. He summoned Mum to her pad and pencil on Sunday morning, as Gan stood stonily at the sink with a bowl of carrots.

The only sounds in the kitchen were her scraping and Mum's scribbling.

It always astonished me how meekly Gan would take Sir Percy's moral strictures. True, Mum always read them out in a grave, "Of course you know this isn't me speaking" voice, but nevertheless, his messages were more often than not, admonishments.

"Come on, m'dear," he gently chided her this time. "Where's that charitable spirit of yours?" Scribble, scribble, and Gan slowly turned round, a half-scraped carrot in her hand.

Sir Percy scribbled some more and Mum gravely read it out. "He says, 'A little tolerance is called for, m'dear. Being right isn't always of the first importance. Remember the fourth Rule of the League . . . Be Loyal One to Another. Your loyalty and understanding are sorely needed just now.'" A humorous note entered Mum's voice, as though she was interpreting the whimsical tenor of his finishing remark. "'I don't need to remind you of the fifth Rule of the League, m'dear'", and he didn't. We all knew it was "OBEY YOUR LEADER".

Mum laid her pad and pencil on the table and looked at Gan. Gan dropped the carrot in the sink behind her and came to the table. "Let's have a cup of tea," she said, her voice gruff to hide her emotion, and it was as though an oppressively heavy wet blanket had been lifted from all of us.

Mum, released from her role of Sir Percy's medium, seemed suddenly vulnerable. She accepted her cup of tea from Gan, then put it down and said, "Oh Mum," a little unsteadily, as though she hardly knew whether to laugh or cry. "I think Sir Percy must have known. I've finished with Sam . . . for good."

Gan immediately stretched out a hand, to pat Mum's shoulder. "Never mind, Ida," she said kindly. "You're better off without him."

Without a sound from any of us children, I think they had forgotten we were there. Mum laughed shakily. "Yes, well . . . we decided it wouldn't work. But you wouldn't credit it . . . he's asked me to send back all his letters and presents."

Gan's expression was a mixture of incredulity and outrage. "Send all his presents back," she exclaimed. "Of all the nerve. Well you don't have to, Ida. They're your property."

Mum said shortly, "I don't want his presents. He's welcome to them."

"Humph," Gan snorted. "Well, it'll puzzle you to give him back his eggs and cream." That drew a smile from Mum, who sighed, "I'll sort out his letters this afternoon."

Gan gave her an earnest stare. "If I were you, Ida, I wouldn't let him have his letters back. You can see what he's afraid of."

Mum looked puzzled. "What?"

"He's afraid you'll sue him for breach of promise. Let him stew for a bit." She looked at Diane and me, as we tried to look as though we weren't listening. "Well, if his Lordship wants your mother's presents back he can have your's too," she said. "Go and fetch them."

So Jill brought the doll Sam had given her for Christmas and Diane brought *Tales of the Arabian Nights*. I lagged behind them with my Christmas present together with my recent birthday gift from Sam, filled with trepidation.

I put the toy sewing machine on the kitchen table beside the silver cross and chain. "I'm sorry," I faltered, as Gan silently surveyed them. "The sewing machine jammed when I got some material stuck in it, and the bit with the needle is broken. And the chain snapped when I tried to get it over my head without unfastening it. I" . . . I stopped breathing, waiting for Gan's angry outburst.

It never came. Instead, she smiled and my alarm changed to confusion. Why was she looking at me with a kind of approval?

Then I realised she must be remembering Sir Percy's plea for tolerance, and was practising it on me.

CHAPTER
NINETEEN

*"When you feel tired of your old clothes remember
that by making them do you are contributing some
part of an aeroplane, a gun or a tank"*

(President of the Board of Trade, Oliver Lyttelton)

Christmas in 1944 was a miserable one. The
Government had promised in October that there would
be extra rations for Christmas, but Gan still had no
heart for it. "What's the good of an extra half-pound of
marge and sugar," she demanded. "What does he
expect us to do with it?" She meant Lord Woolton.

Mum pointed out, "It's an extra half-pound each,"
but all she got was a scornful, "And what am I to make
with it, with no extra dried fruit?"

The only thing which made us feel the war would
soon be over was a relaxation of the blackout, though it
only partially applied to coastal areas. We had what was
called a dim-out and were told our curtains must be
thick enough to prevent forms inside from being seen
from the outside. That incensed Gan too. "What do
they think we're going to do . . . flaunt ourselves to
passing aircraft," she sneered.

There was a critical shortage of coal, and people
were again asked to share their fires with friends. But

we had none that Christmas. Mrs Shipley and Peter had gone to London to stay with relatives and Gan and Mrs Crisp had fallen out again though we still went to watch Mr Crisp march in the Home Guards' standing-down ceremony.

Things got no better in the New Year. Heavy snow covered the whole of the South-West and though there was a quick thaw in February, frost had damaged the crops. For the first time, even potatoes were scarce. Our rations had also been cut because of the need to contribute food to people starving in Europe.

I left school as soon as I was fourteen, to start work as a junior clerk in Oxo Limited in Plymouth. Mum and Gan looked through my last year's summer dresses, all out-grown except for the seersucker dress from Auntie Thelma, with its huge hem and let-outable chest gussets. Out came the sewing machine and Mum let insertions into my bodices and bands into my skirts, cut from an old tablecloth. And Diane, Jill and I all had a new dress for Easter, made from our own material by a woman Mum knew who took in dressmaking.

Clothes-making was strictly controlled by the Government. Pockets on blouses were banned, sleeves had to be narrow, collars and cuffs and the number of pleats in skirts were restricted, and turn-ups on men's trousers were forbidden. I badly wanted pleats cascading from a tight waist for my dress, but Mrs Woolley was adamant.

"I daren't do it, maid," she told me earnestly. "I'd be in trouble if I was found out. Two pleats back and front is as much as I can do."

200

Gan said, rather sharply, "Why ever not? It's our material."

"That don't make no difference," said Mrs Woolley firmly. "Didn't you read about that Plymouth tailor in the paper? He gave a customer four pockets and turnups on his trousers and made I don't know how many skirts with too many pleats . . . and that was with the customers' own material. He was fined ten shillings on every single count."

Gan said shortly, "Well, who's to know? We're not going to tell anyone." Her colour was heightening, always a bad sign. Mum and I exchanged uneasy glances.

Mrs Woolley's colour began to rival Gan's. "And how am I to explain one of my customers decked out in enough pleats to go round two bodies?" she retorted. "Somebody'd shop me, that's for sure. People haven't got any sense of loyalty these days. They'd drop you in it as soon as look at you."

Alarm at Gan's expression made Mum and I both speak together. "I'm sure Mrs Woolley knows best," Mum began, while I blurted out, "I've changed my mind anyway. Just two pleats will be fine."

I knew by Gan's glare that she felt we had let her down, but for once I didn't care. My new yellow dress was assured, with its buttoned bodice and a belt I could tighten whenever Gan wasn't looking and so palpably not that hallmark of growing girls, a renovated garment.

Oxo Limited was situated in the bombed-out centre of Plymouth, though its building had escaped,

That hallmark of growing girls,
The renovated garment.

unscathed. The firm had just returned from its evacuation to Wadebridge, where it had been located in the premises of the Managing Director's farm there.

Gan not only took me for my initial interview, she went in with me. She and Mr Dennison maintained an animated conversation for the whole of my interview and I can't recall saying one word. So I think she must have been right when she said to me on the way to the bus-stop, her face rosily flushed, "Well! How about that for getting-off with a Managing Director? I got that job for you, young woman."

That job opened up a whole new world for me. My weekly wage was £1, to be raised to twenty-five shillings when I eventually gained promotion from Office Junior to Invoice Clerk. I had to make tea, carry messages, usually between offices but sometimes to the depot at Pennycomequick, and also to frank the mail each day. Best of all, I joined a group of people about whom I could form my own opinions, without them first being filtered through Gan.

Apart from Mr Dennison and half-a-dozen travellers, there was only one male in the office. He was a young man taken on during the evacuation to Cornwall, who travelled to Plymouth from Lostwithiel every day. The rest were all female, mostly girls a few years older than me, who typed invoices and kept ledgers, along with several older senior clerks.

I settled in very quickly. Most of the staff were kind and routine was fairly lax in those heady days leading up to VE Day.

Food shortages were still prominent in everyone's minds, and with any rumour of something special coming into the shops, oranges, onions and once, lipsticks, a number of girls, always including me, were sent out to get what we could. With our desks facing the large window overlooking Tavistock Road, one or another of us always saw when an ice-cream queue began to form outside a shop, and were instantly sent off to join it.

We didn't see a great deal of Mr Dennison. He arrived late and left early each day, to and from his farm in Wadebridge. He always gave us a punctilious "Good Morning" or "Goodnight" as he passed through the main office, with a keen glance over us from beneath bushy grey eyebrows. He was a very tall man, stiff and slow-moving, rather intimidating to most of us. When I looked at him I could hardly believe he had brought a blush to my grandmother's cheeks.

Not long after I started work at Oxo I saw, but thankfully did not then have to join, the annual procession of people going in to Mr Dennison's office to ask for a rise. It happened every year without fail. Nobody got a rise without having to ask for it though he always gave us one.

This time, Sally, one of the invoice clerks, came out red-faced to send in the next nervous supplicant.

"What mood is he in?" whispered Nora. "Mean," Sally hissed. "He asked why I thought I should have a rise so I said the cost of living had gone up. 'No it hasn't', he said. 'You can still buy Oxo cubes for a penny each.' "

204

"So you didn't get a rise, then?"

"Yes, half-a-crown," Sally muttered quickly, as a loud, deep voice bellowed from Mr Dennison's room, "Is the next one coming or not?"

He must have forgotten that we were allowed to buy Oxo cubes cash sale for three-farthings each, otherwise Sally might have had to settle for less.

The younger girls didn't have a great deal to do with the older women, except for Miss Fresham, whose eccentricity forced us to notice her. She regularly burped, then immediately loudly berated the person standing nearest to her. "Betty, how could you?" she first accused me and I was overcome with embarrassment until eventually accepting her behaviour as the other girls did. She did it so often, she must have had a dreadful digestion.

Gan was quite disgusted when I told her. "Fancy a woman of her age being so rude," she exclaimed, until I later passed on the story everyone in the office knew, that Miss Fresham had lost her fiancé in the Great War. Gan's attitude changed immediately. "Well, that accounts for a lot," she said sympathetically. "Losing her man does funny things to a woman."

Several of the older girls were waiting for young men to come back from the war and most of their colleagues avidly listened to their hopes and fears, when would their men come home, how soon could they get married and, sometimes, would Bob or Jimmy still love them.

The exception was Margaret, who had such a smug air of confidence and superiority, she aroused catty reactions even in easy-going Sally.

Margaret's fiancé was a naval officer who, she told us, came from a very good family, his father being a solicitor. "Claude is going to study law when he is demobbed," she said. "Then he'll eventually become a partner in his Father's firm."

"So you'll need to keep your job on after you're married," Sally suggested. "Until he's qualified."

"Oh no," Margaret smiled complacently. "There's plenty of money in Claude's family. His parents will support us. And their house is large enough for us to have a flat of our own after we're married."

Margaret brought in a photo of herself to show us, which she was sending to Claude. It was in colour, professionally tinted as colour films were not then available.

Sally, Nora and I sat eating our sandwiches, after Margaret had gone home for lunch.

"What did you think of Margaret's photo?" Nora asked. "I think it'll give Claude something to look forward to, won't it. He hasn't seen her for three years. He'll think she's turned into Hedy Lamarr."

"Only she hasn't, has she," Sally grinned. "What's he going to think when he sees that pasty face with blackheads, and a couple of stones more of her than when he went away? Poor Claude. He's a real good looker, too." We had all seen Margaret's photo of the serious looking young man in his Naval uniform, seated facing the camera, a smile just curving his lips.

Margaret sent her photo off and came into the office a week or so later to announce triumphantly, "Claude's asked me to fix the wedding date. He'll be home on leave at the end of the month."

206

Sally said, "And what did he think of your photo?"

"I think that's what tipped the balance." There was only one word to describe Margaret's smile — superior. "He says he can't wait to call me his own." She loftily ignored the loud burp which exploded from Miss Fresham and its accompanying, "Margaret! I'm surprised at you," to seat herself with dignity at her ledger.

A few weeks later, Margaret came in with the news that Claude was home and was coming to meet her outside the office when she finished work.

From half-past five onwards, Margaret watched for Claude from the office window, until with a pleased little cry, she saw him and sprang up from her ledger. "I'll bring him up to introduce him," she promised. She returned, proudly ushering Claude in, to remove his cap and beam on us all.

If Margaret's photo had given a false impression, so had Claude's. It had not shown how very tall he was, with long, thin hands attached to bony wrists which seemed to emerge endlessly from his cuffs. Now cap-less and viewed from the side, both his hair and his chin were seen to recede and his complexion was as pale as Margaret's. He also displayed the same air of superiority in the little speech he made us.

"On behalf of my fiancée and myself, I'd like to thank you for the support you've given her while I've been away," he began. "I'm sure it helped her through all her worries about me." He paused to give his fiancée a fond look before continuing, "And now, of course, she has nothing more to worry about. We shall soon be man and wife."

We dutifully offered our congratulations, with Sally finishing off for us all with a good-humoured, "I think you really deserve one another". By the satisfied smiles Margaret and Claude exchanged, we knew they agreed with her.

A number of the girls always went to a British Restaurant for lunch every Friday and after a while I went with them. Mum gave me eight shillings and sixpence a week out of my pound. Five shillings was for myself, the other three shillings and sixpence covered my ferry and bus fares.

I could easily afford the Friday meal out, which always cost less than a shilling. My favourite meal was corned beef fritters. It had never occurred to me that corned beef could be so exciting. Gan invariably surrounded hers with potato and carrot, and frequently buried it under a thick coating of pastry.

It had never occurred to me that corned beef
could be so exciting.

208

For the first few weeks I spent every penny of my five shillings, until Gan insisted I should be saving some of it. So I bought a half-crown Savings Stamp every other week and used the money for Christmas and birthday presents, instead of making them.

Mum and Gan must have been relieved. They had a drawer full of the needle-cases, tray-cloths and kettle-holders we usually gave them.

Sally had a boyfriend called Gavin, who was very good at "getting things", though she was always a little vague as to where he got them. She was very generous with what he gave her, though none of us were too clear as to what to do with the yards of surplus blackout material she shared among us. "It would make a nice quilt cover," suggested Miss Fresham. "I could embroider white daisies on it." Mum and Gan accepted my share of it with suitable gratitude, the wartime instinct still strong in them, of never refusing anything which might be useful.

A parachute divided amongst us was much more acceptable, most of the girls declaring it would make lovely cami-knickers.

One day Sally brought in a pile of what looked like plans of engines drawn on pieces of stiff parchment-like material. "It washes out," she assured us. "Then you have this lovely soft linen, and you can make all sorts with it. My Aunt Vera crocheted hers together and it made a lovely tablecloth."

Mum was alarmed when she saw mine. "If anyone catches us with them, they'll think we're spies," she exclaimed. "They look like aeroplane plans."

"Why on earth should they be looking for spies now," Gan said impatiently. "The war's nearly over. Anyway, I'll get them in the wash before anyone sees them."

The size took some washing out and Gan got fed up with the effort. The resulting pile of limp, fraying bits of rag eventually disappeared, before any of us had thought what to make with them.

Sally read a letter in a women's magazine one day, in which a reader enthused about a blouse which she had renovated. Apparently full of holes and tears, she had neatly darned them all, then over each darn she had embroidered a butterfly. Everyone who saw her wearing it, she wrote, had exclaimed at how pretty it was.

Sally was enthusiastic. "I've got an old, white cotton blouse. I'll have a go at that." The following week, she came into work wearing it.

It wasn't exactly pretty ... more unusual. The winged creatures adorning her were too big for butterflies. "That's all right," she said cheerfully. "They're birds. I couldn't do butterflies."

Nora asked, "How did your blouse get worn through in those particular places?" She meant, in the middle of each breast.

"It didn't," said Sally. "It actually got worn under the arm, where blouses always get worn." She lifted her arms, to show large, darned areas beneath them. "But what's the use of putting embroidery where it doesn't show?"

She had a point, though it didn't tie up with her next remark. She said thoughtfully, "But I'll have another go at some smaller ones. I'll do them on my parachute cami-knicks."

CHAPTER
TWENTY

"Something nasty in the woodshed"

(From Stella Gibbons's Cold Comfort Farm*)*

Now well into adolescence, I was becoming acutely conscious of my own femaleness. I was very aware of the sharp divide between men and women, though my experience so far had been very one-sided, growing up as I had in an entirely female family.

I knew that mens' bodies looked different to womens', but had no concept of how much until one dark, late afternoon, when I was coming home from my job in Plymouth on Torpoint ferry. Idly curious, I looked through a porthole into the engine room and, like Aunt Ada Doom, in *Cold Comfort Farm* who saw something nasty in the woodshed, I was never the same again.

It actually was not as much nasty, as an absolute shock. A man was standing beside one of the heavily riveted, watertight doors, completely naked except that his whole body was covered with a mass of dark, curly hair.

It had never occurred to me that men had so much body hair. Up to then I'd only known about male arm-hair, glimpsed when Sam had once rolled up his

I looked through a porthole into the engine room.

shirt sleeves one hot afternoon when he had been courting Mum.

This one looked like a gorilla, so different from the female bodies I was used to seeing, he seemed to me like a creature from another species. I stared, incredulous, until suddenly realising he might look up and see me, I moved hastily away from the porthole and went to wait with other passengers on the front prow of the ferry.

I could not wait to tell everyone when I got home. Diane and Jill were very impressed. I do not know that Mum was, but Gan saw the incident as yet another example of my shortcomings.

"Trust you," she said sharply. "If there's anything that shouldn't be looked at, trust you to look at it!"

"Yes, but . . . " I still had not got over the shock. "It was all over everywhere!"

Mum said kindly, "It was because he was so dark, Betty. Dark-haired men always seem much more hairy than fair-haired ones," then finished off lamely, as she caught Gan's hard stare . . . "I should think."

I never learned anything about sex from Mum and Gan, only a stern warning from Gan that men were either dangerous or rotters, or both, and that girls had always to be on their guard, though she did not explain what against. I first learned about sex from the girls at Oxo. One, in particular, who at nineteen was five years older than me, had an apparently endless fund of knowledge.

Sally found out one day that I had no idea what "making love" entailed.

214

They could not possibly have done such things! *Surely!*

"Well, it's kissing, isn't it?" I said tentatively, and at her amused expression bravely added, "And touching . . . isn't it?"

So Sally told me what marriage entailed and how babies were made, and I just could not believe it. For some reason, my first thought was of Mr and Mrs Crisp. They could not possibly have done such things, surely!

I did not feel able to share this particular new-found knowledge with Mum and Gan, but of course I told

Diane. It was just like when we were seven and eight, when I told her there was no Santa Claus. She refused to believe me then, as she did now. "Sally was making it all up," she told me brusquely.

I brought out my trump card. "Then how do women get babies? How do the babies get in?" It suddenly occurred to me that I still did not know how they got out.

"It's with kissing," but Diane was beginning to sound unsure. "Special kissing."

"It's not! But if you don't believe me . . ." I shrugged my shoulders and left her to think. Just like the Santa Claus argument, when we had been walking home from school down Blindwell Hill, and she had eventually reluctantly demanded, "Well, who gives us the presents then?" she said now, "Do you mean all married people? Even the Crisps?"

Poor Mr and Mrs Crisp would have been horrified had they known of our sexual interest in them. It was because they were so unlikely a couple. Mrs Crisp was very dignified, rather fussy and very ladylike, while Mr Crisp, at first imbued with a little of the prestige which khaki gave, had now lost his uniform with the disbanding of the Home Guard and was again the diffident, dapper little man of pre-hostilities, always under his wife's thumb. Surely she did not let him do *that* to her!

The war continued to dominate our lives, though it seemed more remote now that the bombing had ended. We still regularly listened to the BBC news bulletins, taking heart as the Allies fought their way across

Europe, getting nearer and nearer to Germany, that the war would soon be over.

But the last months dragged out. People got short-tempered and fell out over petty things, especially Gan.

Mrs Shipley had returned home from London with Peter. Gan met her one day, on her way down the stairs with a bucket of pigswill. Gan looked at Mrs Shipley's grey pin-striped pinafore dress. "That's very smart," she smiled. "Did you get it in London?"

Mrs Shipley chuckled. "Not a bit of it, Mrs Cooper. I'll have you know, this was a pair of John's old trousers when I went to the Make-do-and-Mend Circle last week."

Gan was very impressed. "That Mrs Elliot must be a good dressmaker," she remarked. "You wouldn't think so, from the way she's always turned out."

"No, she's left," explained Mrs Shipley. "And you'll never guess who's running the class now ... Mrs Crisp!"

There was a small pause before Gan said, "Mrs Crisp? I didn't know she knew anything about dressmaking."

"She's jolly good, much better than Mrs Elliot. She's got some clever ideas too. Mrs Jackson came in with her old blackout curtains and went home with two dirndl skirts for her girls. Mrs Crisp suggested the girls embroider flowers on the basques, to give them a bit of style. I bet there'll be a few more blackouts coming in next week."

Gan had lost her initial inclination to talk. "Well, don't let me keep you," she said, eyeing Mrs Shipley's bucket of potato peelings. "You don't want to miss the swill collection."

Mrs Crisp's triumph had annoyed her, though she started on Mrs Shipley first.

"You should see the rammel she's wearing," she told Mum. "She didn't need to tell me it was made from her husband's old trousers. You could see his front opening, down the middle of her chest.

"And as for Madam Crisp lording it over the Make-do-and-Mend Circle . . . I saw her yesterday, full of her old buck and laid out like lamb and lettuce. You can't tell me she ever wears renovated garments! That suit she had on must have taken half her hen-pecked old man's coupons, never mind her own. Running the women's sewing group? I tell you, that's a recipe for trouble in the Amen Corner if ever there was one!"

She must have been really incensed, with three of her sayings in one outburst, none of them making any literal sense, but we all knew exactly what she meant.

It was the Amen Corner one that really intrigued me. So I asked her, "Where is the Amen Corner?" She glared at me. "Well, where do you think it is?" she snapped. "In the Bible, of course." I didn't dare pursue it.

Then, came that magic day when Germany surrendered, and people were once again sharing their joy with strangers in the street.

VE Day, on 8th May, was a national holiday, and it was filled with excitement from beginning to end. We

218

hung out the flag we had been keeping in readiness, and listened to Winston Churchill's broadcast, and also to the king's. Church bells rang and the flag-dressed ships in the harbour sounded their hooters.

A bonfire party was planned in the Square near the ferry and when it was dark we all made our way there. Diane, Jill and I wore our new dresses, and behind Gan's back as she walked ahead with Mum and Jill, I pulled my belt in as tight as I could, making the rest of me, above and below it, satisfyingly prominent.

I had bought a bottle of "Instant Stockings", but had no need to use it. A packet of newspapers had arrived from Auntie Thelma and rolled inside the pages, to avoid Customs Duty, were nylons for us all, the first we had seen. We wore them with our latest shoes, heavy and noisy, with thick wooden wedge soles.

In Fore Street we met Mr and Mrs Crisp, and Gan and Mrs Crisp greeted one another with such pleasure, it was as though their quarrel had never happened.

Mrs Crisp was regretting her A.T.S. daughter's inability to get leave, her son's long-overdue liberation from his prisoner-of-war camp, and Mr Crisp's loss of his Home Guard uniform.

"He should have been wearing it today, of all days," she lamented, ignoring the gentle, demurring sounds coming from Mr Crisp.

Gan stoutly reassured her. "He doesn't need his uniform. He looks every inch the man he is, without it," while Diane and I exchanged secret, significant glances.

When we reached the Square, the bonfire was alight, an effigy of Hitler on the top of it. A band was playing dance music, and as we stood watching, a sailor came and drew me into the crowd of dancers.

It was not long before my initial excitement died away. What with my over-tight belt and the sailor's clinching hold on me, I could scarcely breathe. And the breaths I did manage to gasp in were alcohol laden. I realised my partner was the worse for drink and in a turn of the dance managed to shake him off. Thankfully, I scurried back to my family.

Despite Sally's best efforts, I still did not know it all. After telling Mum and Gan how drunk the sailor had been I added indignantly, "And I'm sure the bottle of beer was still in his pocket. I could feel it digging into me all the time we were dancing."

It was too dark to see Mum and Gan's faces, but I could tell by Gan's exasperated sigh that, in some way, I had again annoyed her.

She said to Mum, "*You'll* have to talk to her this time." Then, to my complete mystification, she snapped at me, "It's your own fault, you silly little madam! I *told* you that pulling yourself in like that would land you in trouble."

I stared, trying to make out her expression in the fire-glow. Then suddenly, it seemed as though every ship in the Dockyard, and all those in the Sound, sounded their sirens in unison, searchlights flooded the sky above us and everybody burst into a spontaneous cheer, and I gave up trying to fathom how my tight belt could be blamed for a drunken sailor and joined in.

Also available in ISIS Large Print:

There's Trouble in the Tea-Leaves

Betty Kellar

Betty Kellar grew up with her two sisters and widowed mother under the watchful eye of her grandmother, whose indomitable spirit held the family together through poverty and war. Their little village of Millbrook, on the Cornish border, was still extremely isolated in the early years of the Second World War. But it was only five miles from Plymouth as the bomber flies.

Kellar tells of the village women and their robust attitudes, their fall-outs over petty issues and their solidarity during times of trouble; of school life, where both children and teachers were deeply committed to the War effort. And through it all "Gan" holds her own, whether it be against Hitler, a flock of belligerent geese, or her feuding neighbours.

ISBN 0-7531-9802-9 (hb)
ISBN 0-7531-9803-7 (pb)

86 Smith Street

Joan Park

A memoir that recaptures ordinary family life in 1930s Britain

Daughter of a ship steward and a housewife, Joan Park gives a delightful glimpse of her childhood from 1927 to 1941, when she and her family lived at 86 Smith Street in Liverpool.

From the descriptions of her granddad's shoe repair shop to the stories her mother used to tell, Joan Park recounts her personal memories of the time of the Great Depression with a child's innocent eye. This is life as she encountered it in those days — family, friends, school and the little incidents — all of which had a big part to play in the day-to-day life of a little girl growing up in Liverpool.

ISBN 0-7531-9842-8 (hb)
ISBN 0-7531-9843-6 (pb)